THE PLACE

IN

BETWEEN

The Grim Reverend Steven Rage

"Del, a man who, when confronted with evidence that his wife was cheating, unsuccessfully attempts suicide and ends up confined to a wheelchair, unable to speak or even breathe on his own. And then he's released to the care of his cheating wife and her lover. To the outside world, they're a devoted wife and good friend. Privately, they taunt, torment and torture the helpless Del--until a demon shows up to help him. Ah, but it's not quite that simple: Rage starts the story out with the Euripides quote, *"The gods visit the sins of the fathers upon the children."* And Rage weaves this theme into the characters' backstories, giving the story an extra dimension."

~Ray Holland, Amazon Review.

"Del's wife Luci is having an affair with her drug supplier, Sancho. Sancho and Luci eventually manage to get custody of the invalid Del, and Sancho uses this as payback time from their navy days (apparently Del had done something to ruin Sancho's career). The story becomes an extreme torture tale, one that made me wince a few times...but Del manages to turn the tables via a Faust-ish deal with a demon. Rage also gives another fresh spin here on ghosts, making this a perfect blend of hardcore horror and Bizarro goodness."

~Nick Cato, Amazon Review.

"The gods visit the sins of the fathers upon the children."

-EURIPIDES

STATESIDE, 1986

RUSTY KNEW THERE WASN'T GOING TO BE much left of her. She'd been inside Del far too long. She was most likely already more than half-eaten. He waited patiently, staying put in the corner of the bedroom, hiding behind a tiny dust bunny. He'd been there for weeks, maybe months, even. Rusty was single-minded in his concentration. The ghost had to save his step-daughter, Luci from her prison. He had this one mission left to complete. Then, if he succeeded, perhaps all could still be forgiven.

Such an advantage, being a sentient ghost: he could make himself as large or as tiny as he wanted. Rusty was still tiny. As tiny as the dust bunny he was hiding behind.

Rusty had to wait until Del was alone and in a deep sleep before he could attempt another rescue. The girl with the dreadlocks Del had shacked up with concerned the ghost. There was much more to her than met the eye. The ghost had to watch out for her and be very careful. If the girl caught him going after Luci, his goose would be thoroughly cooked. But she was gone right now. This was unusual. It seemed as though the girl never left Del. Rusty wondered where she went.

Del was sleeping by himself on the bed but the sleep was restless. The ghost would have to wait until Del was deeper down the rabbit hole of sleep than that. Rusty would have to stay tiny and take no chances. Being so small was actually a great boon to the ghost, one that he would try to use to his supreme advantage.

Finally, the ghost could hear Del's breathing change. It lengthened and softened. The air entered slowly and left just as placidly. Now Del was deep enough for the ghost to go inside of him and hunt for Luci.

The ghost grew a little larger in size. He needed to make it across the carpet before daylight brought the sun shining through the window. He couldn't have Del awaken before helping Luci escape. Rusty ran from the dust bunny that now stood no taller than his ankles. Then he darted from a dirty sock to a musky pair of panties to the edge of the bed. The ghost climbed the comforter, scaling the mattress mountain range quickly.

Rusty hid briefly behind a rolling hillock of bed sheets, detecting no movement. Del was still breathing evenly – still sleeping soundly. The ghost crept along the periphery of Del's giant outline. He was seeking the healed and closed stoma in Del's belly. Del lay on his left side so that his stoma opening was now just a touch above the ghost's head. Rusty grew himself a wee bit more in order to face the hole squarely. He took two fingers on his right hand and forced them through Del's coarse and sticky scar tissue. The colon gas whistled out, whipping in a brief fury the ghost's hair in a stinky wind. He was dead already, so any stink less than his own completely bypassed the ghost. He knew this might hurt the sleeping man. The hole the ghost was making was small, but he couldn't take any chances of Del awakening in mid-rescue.

When Del didn't budge an inch, the ghost leaned in to him. He pushed his hand all the way into the healed scar tissue. He ignored the small leak of liquefied stool that splashed his arm, all the way up to the elbow. He slid in the other hand and pulled the hole open enough for the ghost to slip in. First he pushed his head in and then, gaining purchase on the inside of Del's abdominal cavity, he pulled himself the rest of the way in.

The ghost stood up inside of Del's thick, spongy colon and looked all around. He had no idea how he would find Luci, but he knew she was in here somewhere. Rusty saw it happen. Luci had to be someplace nearby. He called out to her, but she didn't answer. Not knowing what else to do, the ghost began walking. Right down the middle of a nice straight section of Del's lower intestine, searching frantically for her. Hoping against hope she wasn't already gone; that nothing remained of beautiful Luci.

Rusty grew out a fingernail until a long sharpened length emerged. As a nervous tic, he began to re-open the scars on his chest. The blood fell in drippy sheets as he went along Del's lower colon, his feet squish-sucking, desperately seeking Luci. He was hoping against hope that when he did finally locate her, she was more than just a big old pile of her bones.

Wishful thinking.

THE DREAD-LOCKED GIRL WAS SITTING MINISCULE and cross-legged on a red blood cell, enjoying a magic carpet ride.

She rode Del's veins, stopping where the blood drains into his gastrointestinal tract.

She left the blood vessel and dropped down into the sleeping man's colon. She landed on her feet with a squish.
The girl fell in to a lock-step behind the ghost. She had known this ghost for decades now, long before Rusty had died.

The two of them had some business to conclude that was long overdue. She had followed him as he began this quest for his long-estranged step-daughter. However, Rusty had her to reckon with first.

The ghost was surprised. He thought he had escaped the dread-locked girl, but she wasn't finished with Rusty yet.

Not by a long shot.

Her eyes began to glow red as she reached for him.

EIGHT MONTHS EARLIER….

ONE

DELANO SAT AT ATTENTION. He was sitting up straight and tall on the very edge of his bed. He held a target loaded .45 and waited for his cheating wife to come home. The five shot ball loaded clip-fed gun felt both heavy and comfortable in his sweaty hand.

She's going to like this one, he thought. The dog-fucking coke-whore is going to get a real kick out of it.

The camos Del wore as the Ordinance Safety Officer at the pistol range were rolled up to his elbows. He stared at the forever tattoo on the underside of his forearm. He had it inked for his and Lucita's fifth wedding anniversary. It used to be Del's favorite one. It had beautiful lines and vibrant colors. The tattoo seemed trite and ridiculous now.

The cleaning kit sat open on the deck between his boots. The gun oil and brushes dropped as he'd used them. There was no more need to be his usual meticulous and methodical self. As a career Navy man, Del took a big chance sneaking the gun off the base. He knew he'd be in deep shit if he ever got caught with the range pistol. It was not like him at all. Del usually chose the straight and narrow path. He was everything that his father – the Sergeant – was not. He didn't do drugs and he didn't drink to excess. He never raped or tortured anyone. Del's father could not say the same. His old man had been involved in both the My Lai and Co Luy fiascos. He served, apparently with a certain cold, cruel distinction, under the now infamous Lieutenant Rusty. And although the sergeant never had to serve any prison time for the murders committed, he had also showed little remorse for his actions. He had even visited the lieutenant in the brig a few times over the years – the disgraced officer was probably still rotting in a jail somewhere. Or maybe he was dead. Del didn't know and he didn't care to keep track. The sergeant himself had died a number of years ago. Near the end, there was nothing much left of Del's father. He left this world a burnt out, drugged up, shell of his former self. It was quite poetic, really.

The Sergeant's myriad sins had absolutely nothing to do with Del and the life of honor he'd built for himself and Luci. That's part of why his wife's indiscretions hurt him so much. Del had tried his whole life to do the right thing. He wanted to re-establish the family line of distinguished career Navy men. Del wanted to be like his grandfather and his grandfather's father. He wanted to follow the rules and be the good guy. Del joined the Navy and happily did everything right and above board. He wanted to be the polar opposite of his father, the baby killer. Del wanted to be the man who returned honor and respect back to the family name.

So, after all he'd been through, after repeatedly bending over backwards for that bitch-twat of a junkie-ass wife of his, being sent those horrible pictures pushed Del off the bow and into the deep drink. A bullet seemed to be the only answer.

He looked to the pistol again, still not believing that he was actually holding the illegal firearm.

It wasn't supposed to ever leave the range, but Del needed it.

He was waiting for her to come home, so he could harm her in the surest way he knew how.

Del had never done anything like this before. Breaking the rules wasn't in his character. But neither was looking the other way while Luci fucked that piece of shit. Not for the cocaine he gave her. Hell, not for any reason. It wasn't just her indiscretions that got on Del's tits. It was him. Sancho was a fucking derelict! Beautiful Luci was cheating on Del with a can't-hack-it, fucking washout. The guy was a huge flake. One who got booted out of the Navy, but stuck around the periphery. He preyed on weaknesses like Luci's love for cocaine.

Del had hidden their assets from her a long time ago, so she couldn't bankrupt them again. This wasn't her first rodeo. He had sent her to rehab again. Then he requested an emergency transfer to shore duty. The Navy takes care of its own. They sent Del from West Pac to the East Coast. Far enough away, Del had thought. And she had been good for a while; a handful of years, in fact. Then that monkey-fuck Sancho found her.

Del wondered how that had happened. He was curious as to just exactly how they had met. What the circumstances had been. He had thought she was being good and behaving herself. But he wasn't going to ask her. He didn't want to hear her lie again. No matter. Del knew how it would go. Just like the other times in the past. One line would lead to twelve and soon she would be sucking on a crack pipe, like she was sucking on the derelict's dick.

He knew that last part was already happening. He wished he didn't know about the affair. Sancho made sure Del knew. Sancho hated the Navy that kicked him out and all who thrived in it like Del, so you can bet he made sure Del knew all about it.

> *"Ouch, baby, it hurts..."*
> *"Do you want me to stop?"*
> *"No, Daddy. Please, no..."*

Then the rat-fucking bastard actually turns to the lens and winks. The only thing missing was the sordid, off-camera details.

This washout wanted to humiliate Del. There was no other reason to send him those nasty pictures. Luci did not even look like she knew she was being filmed. And Sancho took care to ensure Del knew the cock she was bouncing on was his. Del knew who Sancho was, alright. There was no way he'd be able to forget. Del was hoping Sancho had been put away for good, but guess not. It looked to Del like the motherfucker was back.

Well, that's just terrific, Tom! And judging from that exclusive film clip, Del's wife appears to be on a liquid diet, as well. She sure does seem to enjoy it, Tom! Fantastic!

It was too much for Del to handle. He couldn't – strike that – Del wouldn't go through that shit with her again.

God damn them. God damn them both.

Del heard Luci's key engage the lock on the front door. He should still be at the Naval Station, but he kind of ran the little show there at the pistol range. Del could cut out early, the .45 notwithstanding, without any issue. He just never did. Today, however, was a special occasion.

"Hey, honey," Del heard himself say. Of course she was startled a little. At least she was by herself. That was something. Del wanted this to be a private affair. Affair, Del chortled. What a word. It sounded so painless.

"You home, Del?" Luci called out, stating the obvious and shutting the door.

Del laughed low and smiled cruelly, shaking his head.

"Yeah, I'm home," he said.

And ain't you the fucking genius.

Del heard Luci making her way back to the bedroom. He put the .45 between his legs and waited.

Del looked overhead, staring at the tiny cracks and imperfections in the ceiling that he had never noticed before. Just like the first handful of times Luci had pulled this shit. He was done overlooking all the flaws and blemishes in their travesty of a marriage. He was sick of this shit; tired of letting it go. Del would make double-damned sure she would pay for this one. Dearly. When Del was done with her, she'd never do it again. He squeezed the solid butt of the pistol with a death-grip. He began to shake, but only a little.

I'm going to show you I mean business, Luci, dearest. I'm gonna press the no-bullshit end of this gun right into the flawless flesh of your forehead, Del thought wickedly. Yeah, sugar-pop, make you feel it. Make you sweat a little. And then? Two quick pops, baby, right between your beautiful blue eyes.

TWO

LUCI STOOD WITH HER LEGS APART in the shower stall. The motel room Sancho got for them was only a few miles from base, but far enough away to keep Del from knowing about it. She hoped. Luci knew he'd kick her ass if she was discovered fucking around on him again. But Sancho gave her uncut virgin shit. The most potent crack she had ever smoked. She'd shake the vial until she heard the rock form. It clink-clinked around and it'd make her wet. And then when she was high, all she wanted to do was fuck. Sancho was, after all, very handsome.

Luci had seen him for the first time at the Tier II brig. He was striking. Even though Sancho looked like he'd been to hell and back. She saw him coming out as she was going in. Despite being underweight, covered with bruises and a couple of chipped teeth, Luci was blown away. Sancho was a wounded bird and Luci definitely had the wounded bird syndrome. The beaten young man looked downtrodden and lost, but he still smiled a huge, charming smile when he saw her in the out-processing area. Seeing him looking so forlorn made the maternal side of her swell. Luci was coming to sign the paperwork so the military could bury her 'father'. Well, sort of a de-facto step-father, he was sandwiched between her mother's 18th and 20th boyfriend out of 30 or 40 something dudes before her mother finally died years ago. Luci didn't know why Rusty chose her as the next of kin.

"You have girlfriend, Vietnam Joe?"

"Don't need one, little yella sista. This dumb bitch left us with her little tight daughter right here. She's only half-gook, but slanty enough to get the job done."

Maybe he still held on to those woefully pleasant memories of gang-raping her when she was young.

Her mom would be gone somewhere – usually at work. Rusty would get himself nice and liquored up and call over some friends. Then he would take her down to the basement.

Rusty would shed his clothes, the criss-crossed scars on his chest shining pale white against his red flushed muscle and skin. He and his buddies would run trains on Luci like she was some gook whore they were having fond fevered memories of.

Luci finished squeezing the store-bought douche up her vagina, trying to rinse Sancho's seed out of her. Vague bad memories of telling her mother about being raped by Rusty and his buddies pushed their way to the front of Luci's mind. Showing her how to douche properly was her mother's only response when she told her about the attacks. They were bad memories, for sure. But that mean old bastard finally died. She had the paperwork to prove it.

Luci was going to surprise Del with the proceeds of the life insurance she was sure Rusty would have left for her, but there was nothing. Rusty left her only a few bits and pieces of personal effects and not even any retirement benefits. Rusty ended his military prison sentence with a Dishonorable Discharge. He would have lost any benefits Luci might have been entitled to anyway. What a piece of shit. Fucking Rusty. His last act was inconveniencing Luci, without even leaving her anything in return. And when she finally signed all the paperwork and collected his dog tags, she felt the most uncomfortably horrible feeling she'd ever had. Her entire body felt ice-cold and her thinking became muddled. Luci felt like she'd hurt her back. It was like she had twisted it in some weird way because her back never did feel right after that.

Then, for the first time in years, the thought of cocaine became much, much more than the wistful wishes she'd had since rehab. It became a powerful lusting urge that morphed into a full-blown obsession. It happened right there while she was holding Rusty's tags and signing paper work. She left the brig and saw the hang-dog handsome young man waiting for her. Luci felt an instant relief when she saw the former sailor. She just knew he'd be able to help her with her desires. Luci was right on the money. Sancho knew exactly where to go. It turned out to be a very good thing that she'd kept her 30 mile drive secret from Del, after all.

Christ, she thought, still squeezing the douche. Imagine if Sancho knocked me up. Fuck! She knew she should have made Sancho wear a raincoat, but she always got caught up with the crack and the cock. Luci couldn't help it. She tried what she felt was her best to kick the love of cocaine, but its grip on her was fixed tight. She was fine, she had thought, following her months of rehab. But not now. It seemed that these days the monkey clawed at her constantly. She couldn't escape its magnetic pull. Luci realized now that even when she was in rehab, she was merely going through the motions. Luci knew Del would never understand. Hell, maybe he couldn't. He was such a Dudley-fucking Do-Right, he probably couldn't even conceptualize doing anything he wasn't supposed to. He was a Navy man, after all, and he was comfortable toeing a straight line and obeying direct orders. Luci chafed at the very notion.

Out of the shower, Luci dried herself off and got dressed. She waited impatiently for the anti-anxiety pill Sancho had given her to kick in. She couldn't go home and face Del this twisted but luckily Del never came home early.

THREE

SANCHO SAT AT THE TABLE, STARING IDLY through the motel window and out beyond Luci's car.

After he was finally released from the brig, Sancho had persuaded Luci to front him a couple of thousand dollars. Even he was amazed at how quickly she gave it up. All she wanted was to be continually supplied with rocks and to get fucked when she was ready. She had the whole: I've been bad, Papi shit down pat. He didn't care. Whatever she needed to rationalize her slutty behavior, Sancho obliged. It really shouldn't have been so easy, though.

Sancho had experience with tons of bitches like Luci. She was his favorite type, the easiest to manipulate.

He knew just how she wanted it: Luci wanted to be ogled and coveted at first. She wanted the desire for her to be transparent. She wants you to be barely able to contain yourself, and yet she still wants to be treated like a lady. Until she was high enough, that is. Then the foreplay was over and Luci wanted her hair pulled and her ass smacked and to get the dog fucked out of her. Sancho just had to be extremely careful not to bruise her up until he was ready to stir from his perch. And that's why he'd pinked-up her heart-shaped bubble butt with today's session. Luci was so stoned he doubted she'd even notice the lovely bruise-stains he left on her ass. It had given him ideas for later. She could be such an untapped source of income for him.

Regardless of how this future financial venture played out, Sancho was ready to make his big move right now. Years of dreamless scheming were about to culminate. He savored the notion like the first line of nose yum, or a small taste of rare wine.

Sancho sniffed back two lines of coke from the big pile on the table beside him. He looked up and out at the weather, tunelessly humming to himself.

It was drizzling softly out, cloudy and just a little bit chilly. He absently tapped out a rhythm on the big plate of cocaine in front of him. Sancho had an ounce in that pile, if he had a gram. That's what he dipped into. It sat white and promising beside a few rocks of crack drying out for Luci on some paper towels.

Sancho was stoned. He was anxious to get up and check out the recording equipment, but he wasn't taking any chances. He waited until he heard Luci's shower going before moving away from the table. The last two lines of coke were still ringing in his head. He stood and chuckled to himself. Jesus this broad was dumb. She acted like her being so pretty entitled her to whatever she wanted. Including the coke he provided and the cock she serviced. Dumb shit. She had no idea how extraneous she really was. Even being Rusty's kid and a golden money purse, Luci wasn't the main drag. It was a nice bonus, but it was her limp-dick squid husband he was after.

Fucking Navy fuck. He'd show Del a thing or three.

Sancho changed his mind and bent at the waist. He sucked up just one more line and then rose. Making sure she was still showering, he went sniffing to his overnight bag conveniently placed on the night stand. From there, the camera had snapped and filmed all that the coked-out Luci had to offer.

First he would ruin Del's little world. Then embarrass the Navy. Soon everyone would know what an absolute skank Del's wife was. Lastly, when he was through with her, Sancho would make a tidy sum selling her video-taped rolling flesh-toned, half-slope, cum-covered, hills of ass all over and beyond. Thereby killing many birds with one stone.

It made Sancho smile. He'd already sent Luci's husband a few choice pics. He made sure Del saw who was fucking his little angel. And if her old man was ballsy enough to step up to Sancho, he'd hand the sailor his ass. One could only hope.

FOUR

DEL REMEMBERED THIS NEXT PART, right down to the tiniest of details. The sun was shining through the bedroom window and over his shoulder. He could hear Luci as she padded her way down the hallway from the front door. The bright yellow light shone a spot on a spider. It was crazy busy trying to wrap up a bug it had caught. It was a housefly, probably. He sympathized with them both. The spider and the fly were both caught by their own designs and the whims of nature. Both will be dead before long – the fly obviously sooner than the spider – and no one will even know that they had been alive. It was just another travesty of the food chain. Either you eat, or you get eaten. It's as simple as that. Del knew what that was like. He was becoming real acquainted with them. He'd had plenty of life and death questions. They were all mixed up lately with his dangerous revenge fantasies. It took him a while, but he knew what he must do. Oh, boy was he going to school her. Was he ever? You could count on it.

Del heard her as she approached the bedroom door. He saw Luci as she broached the threshold of the doorway. Del opened his legs. He let Luci see the gun. It amused him to no end watching as her fake grin crumbled. She stared at the gun Del held as if fixated by an unbreakable trance. She barely heard him as Del spoke.

"I've had enough of this shit," he told her. Del raised the .45 and leveled it steady at her chest. "More than that, I've had enough of you."

"Del, don't," she said, her eyes locking on his now. Her voice quivered as she spoke and the color drained from her face.

"Bitch, please," he replied wryly. "I'm not going to shoot you," he told her. "I just wanted to get you shook." He lowered the gun. Luci began to cry from the release of the strain. Her hands flew dramatically to her face. It was a crying shame to see her so upset.

"Oh, my God, Del," she said, taking a tentative step toward her armed husband. "For a minute there I thought you really were going to kill me." She stepped closer. "You scared the shit out of me, you jerk," Luci told him, smiling once more. Del smiled back at her.

"I really got to you, huh?"

"Yeah, honey, you really did," Luci replied and stopped right in front of her husband. He cocked his head to the side, peering up at her.

"Well then," he said, "You're really going to get a kick out of this," and he placed the .45 in his own mouth. Time skidded to a stop. As Luci shouted and lunged for him, Del squeezed the trigger.

The blood from the gun shot splattered everywhere.

● ● ● ●

THE POLICE WERE THE FIRST TO ARRIVE ON THE SCENE. They took one look and started rolling out the yellow crime scene tape. Luci had to prove to them that Del was still alive. He had a pulse, but wasn't breathing. The cops called for the emergency services and waited for them to arrive. There was no way they were going to do any mouth-to-gaping-gunshot-wound on him. There was just no way. The fire and ambulance teams arrived in short order. They got Del stabilized, but it was just enough to move him to the military hospital and immediately into emergency surgery. The surgical team had to resuscitate Del three separate times. He was in surgery for hours. Some of the Navy's top surgeons leaning over Del's face and neck, their damp foreheads nearly touching. They were compelled to remove a good portion of the man's face because the bullet had pretty much disintegrated the entire jaw. Bits of bone had fragmented and peppered the wet mucosa. The finer particles of bone dust had been inadvertently sucked into Del's lungs, causing a horrifying and life threatening pneumonia. It began to take so much pressure to oxygenate Del that the doctors had to strap him into a roto-bed. Being constantly turned, Del was rotating like a roasting pig in a luau. Using gravity to manipulate his perfusion, Del was blissfully narcotized and thankfully unaware.

FIVE

IT WAS NEVER NIGHTTIME IN THE ICU. All the machines, the monitors and assorted paraphernalia, along with the chatter of the pros, caused a continuously surreal environment for the patients and workers alike.

Visitors held their loved one's cold hands, staring at all of the indecipherable numbers and squiggles, searching for the truth to their one single-minded thought:

Will they get better?

The demon stood in the middle of the military hospital's Intensive Care Unit and looked all around. He had his hands on his hips. Like a kid in a candy shop, he smiled excitedly. Like a hungry man waiting in line for the all-you-can-eat buffet, the demon was both anxious and pleased. The demon was invisible to everyone still firmly fixed on this side of That. For those that straddled the line, however, the ancient one was clearly seen. For them the demon was a reminder of what was yet to come.

The demon was not here for them. That was some other functionary's job. This evil one had been around since before the Earth cooled and the rib was plucked from Adam's cage. He wasn't here to collect on any past-due notices. The demon was here following its own agenda. He had a marvelous project in mind and was looking for just the right person to help him see it through.

There are many souls here. And ripe they are. So ready for plucking.

He just had to find one that wasn't leaving the trauma ward feet first, but still fucked up enough to barter with.

The demon casually and invisibly strolled up and down the Unit, taking his time, gazing at the traumatized flesh and bone. He had been to this particular ICU many times. It did not matter to the demon much that his many previous trips proved fruitless. The demon was the epitome of patience. Being eons old certainly helped. The demon knew that he had all the time in the world. Being forced to wait like this had heightened the demon's sense of anticipation. The demon walked slowly up and down the Unit. He touched each patient and peeked over the shoulders of the nurses as they charted their thoughts and findings. Each time the demon stopped near one of the nurses, or any of the other staff, they would feel even colder than usual. If he stayed long enough, the staff member would actually exhale a cold plume of frigid air. They would get an almost overwhelming urge to either fuck or punch the first person they saw. The demon was a very bad influence. The staff didn't know it was a Hellion out on a jaunty lark. They would usually blame it on a full moon they could never see from the patient's bed side. With all the pain and trauma stretched out in long, even rows, the demon felt like an affluent gentleman farmer that was surveying his cash crop and gauging its worth. He came to a stop at the foot of the big motorized rotating bed. Pointing his wrinkled leather finger at the screen of the bedside computer, he scrolled down the patient's history. It showed to him everything the demon needed to know. He smiled wickedly.

This sailor was perfect, the demon thought.

SIX

THE PLASTIC PROSTHETIC WAS HARD TO LOOK AT. It was necessary, though, to keep Del's face from collapsing on itself. Other than that it was mostly aesthetic. The face-piece was wired to move so Del could talk, if he'd been able to. However, the bullet also blew through the back of his neck, nearly severing the spinal column at the third vertebra. Del was permanently attached to a mechanical ventilator that breathed for him through the tube placed in his throat. Del could blink and think and that was about it.

Once Del recovered from his more life-threatening conditions, the hospital staff began making arrangements for Luci to take Del home to take care of him. It was going to be a lifetime commitment, but Luci told them all that she didn't mind. She let her raspy voice get all maudlin and her eyes leaked their feigned sorrow. Del wasn't buying it, not for a second. Not that it mattered. No one asked Del's opinion on anything anyway. Because he couldn't communicate, they thought his mind was now just medicated mush. They talked around him, about him, and didn't give it a second thought. Then Sancho started showing up with Luci to visit Del in the hospital. The staff thought Del was sooo lucky to have such a devoted wife and such a solid friend in Sancho. Naturally, as

THE PLACE IN BETWEEN

soon as no one was looking, Sancho and Luci would slip into Del's bathroom and snuffle up some stuff and fondle each other. Del couldn't help but hear everything. He had a bad feeling about going home with those two. But again, no one asked Del his opinion.

It was finally time to send Del off to his new life with a hearty fare-thee-well. They gave Del a puff-n-sip wheelchair, somehow forgetting that he could do neither. Luci and Sancho – Del's good friend – made quite a show of the wheelchair accessible changes made to his home. Everyone was anxiously waiting to leave. No one felt comfortable with the three of them, but the court made their decisions concerning Del's care. Luci and Sancho were it.

The gun shot was written off as an accident which entitled Luci, his legal guardian, several thousand dollars a month in government checks and benefits. All of Del's net worth was joint-owned, technically. Sancho was there to help her liquidate and spend it. They just had to find Del's investments first. They asked him, but it was clearly a no-go. Del wouldn't tell them shit. Even if he could speak, Del would have told them fuck-all.

They wheeled Del up the ramp and through the front door. Sancho parked him in a corner of the living room. He made a great show of fussing over Del. The official visitors were impressed. They ignored the warning alarms blaring in their brain pans. Del, they figured, will do just fine. He has a strong support system in place. He has people to care and look out for him. They were anxious to get underway.

As soon as the representatives from the Department of Defense and VA left their home, Sancho's smile slid away like the promises of an ill-intentioned suitor. He watched as they packed themselves into their government Ford sedans and drove away. They disappeared around the corner and were gone.

Luci sat with a sigh on the couch. She'd thought they were never going to leave.

Sancho then turned with scorn to Del. "So," he began. He quickly made his way over to the wheelchair-bound Del. He continued, "Tell me, boy, just who is the fucking derelict now, big shot?" Sancho asked. Luci chuckled as she loaded her crack pipe. Sancho looked over to her, then back to Del. He said, "I'm going to make your beautiful wife suck on my dick, you fucking squid." Sancho leaned into Del's horrible face. "Right here in front of you. What do you think about that?" Sancho raised his eyebrows, waiting for the response he knew Del could not give. Luci lit the pipe. She said nothing. "I'm going to make you pay for dropping dime on me. Believe that."

Del did.

SEVEN

DEL SAT MOTIONLESS AS SANCHO REMOVED his breathing tube. He was playing a favorite game of his: see how blue the gimp can get. Luci was sitting on the couch nearby, smoking crack and doing her nails. The television was turned on to the shopping network. Periodically Luci would pick up the house phone and order on Del's credit cards some more useless and unneeded trinkets and baubles.

Del could feel himself fading. The clouds began to gather on the horizon of his peripheral vision. His oxygen level was dropping out his ass. He wondered if Sancho hated – or was it liked – him enough to let Del die, right here and now. But it was not to be. Sancho hooked him back up to his hose and breathing machine. Del was disgusted at himself for being grateful. Being tortured and humiliated like this was not easy for Del to swallow. It was a long way down from when he was in the West Pac fleet...

Del was a Second Class Petty Officer manning the Fire Control for the Guided Missile Frigate Kokhring. He loved his gig aboard the F.F.G ship. Del suspected any Navy man would. Shit, his Naval Enlisted Classification entitled Del to launch the motherfucking missiles. And it was cool as shit to watch the birds take off. They launched with so much thrust that the after-burn scorched the paint on the ship's deck all the way down to bare metal. The humps had to paint the deck every time the ship made port.

Del was good at it too. He could launch and park one up a mosquito's ass if he had to. He was looking at making Chief in a couple of short years. He didn't even mind the long deployment stints. Other than being away from Luci (and always wondering what the fuck she was up to) for six long months at a time, Del loved being at sea. He'd been to all the classic West Pac ports of call; Japan, Subic Bay, hell, all over. It was great.

Del recalled the times he went with his shipmates to see the Filipino bar girls. The girls put on quite a show. They could pick up pesos with their snatch and, when the sailor would ask for it, given to him the exact change requested. Then all the rest of the squids would put a dent in their pay by getting their lances waxed. Del would never indulge in that way. He would just sit there and get drunk and watch his friends have at it. He was happily detached, being happily married. Stupid, was how he felt now. All the opportunities to get down and dirty Del had let slip on by. Always telling himself, and pretty convincingly, that Luci was also faithful to him. Del was able to convince himself that she was being a good girl.

Luci sure fucked all that up. Del was grateful, and always would be, for the quick transfer to the pistol range the Navy managed to find for him. It was good duty, but it wasn't sea duty. And without the score of ninety day stars on his Sea Duty Ribbon it would be very difficult for Del to get that Chief's promotion he coveted so.

It all came crashing down when Sancho sent Del the pictures of Luci. How bad was it that it did not matter one whit to Luci that he'd shortchanged his career for her. How embarrassed Del was that he couldn't even control his own wife. That he tried to end his own life. And that he failed to even accomplish that.

Sancho was a piece of shit, no doubt about it, but Del understood why the washout hated Del so much.

Sancho used to be assigned to the pistol range with him. Del had witnessed Sancho selling cocaine and whatever those fucking pills were, while he was on duty. The guy was so stupid and brazen. Well, Del couldn't have that shit going on under his nose and on his watch. So he ducked out and made the call. Shore Patrol got to the pistol range faster than a rabbit gets fucked. That spelled the end of Sancho's short-lived career in the Navy. Sancho was hauled off, court martialed and booted out. Del had thought that was the end of that.

Jesus, was I wrong.

A hard slap from Sancho woke Del up.

"Wakey-wakey, sleepyhead," he ordered. Sancho eyed Del closely. "You got pretty blue that time, almost purple."

Del's head was screaming pain at him from the hypoxia.

That fucking piece of shit, Sancho. God how I hate him. Anything. I would give anything for this to stop.

Del heard Sancho laugh. Luci was coming down now and getting a little woozy. She was staring glassy-eyed at the TV, sitting on the couch with a bong in her lap. She didn't seem to notice what Sancho was doing to Del.

Why, baby? Why do you let this derelict do this to me? You're my wife! Don't you care at all? Don't I mean anything to you?

"Hey, baby?" Luci slurred.

Yes, honey?

"What?" from Sancho. He disconnected Del again.
You're sorry? You're going to make him stop? Can't you see that I am suffering?

"I want a party," Luci replied instead.

A party, you ditzy cunt?!

"What kind of party?"

A fucking party?!

"Yeah, I want a big one," said Luci, emphatically. "With lots of people I don't know. I wanna meet some new people. I want you to show me off. You should invite all your friends, Papi."

Papi? So it's Papi now? Daddy, oh Daddy wasn't enough while you were getting your doughnut punched by him. Now, it's Papi, too.

"Sure, baby," Sancho replied, removing Del's circuit again. "We'll have ourselves a real blowout." Sancho smiled at Del as he struggled for the breath he couldn't get. "Don't feel bad, son, you'll be invited, too," promised Sancho. "It'll be a big hoot." He started laughing at the thought of Del the gimp at a party, any party. "Just wait 'til they get a load of you."

I'm dying and you don't even care...

Del passed out. Sancho's laughter followed him far down into the inky forbidden darkness.

•••

DEL HIT THE HARD-PACKED DIRT FLOOR, landing unceremoniously on his rump. It was both dark as sin and hot as hell down there. The sound of water hissing steam was everywhere. His wheelchair was gone. Del touched his face lightly and he felt real flesh, not plastic. He was standing there, in the dark, but under his own power. He was breathing on his own. The hole in his throat was gone. The hole in his belly was gone. The IVs and catheters too. He could see nothing but darkness all around him. Del was surprised that he was not afraid. He could see, there was some light, but it only surrounded him in his immediate vicinity. He was trapped in a moveable bubble. Not knowing what else to do, Del began walking straight ahead.

As his eyes adjusted to the intense darkness binding him, the outlines of huge marble columns emerged. Del came to and walked through the entrance of a Roman bath house. The bath was further heated by an underground fire, stoked with bits of bark, wood chips and small pieces of kindling. The fire rose ever higher like the prayers of true believers. Veiled human forms feebly emerged as Del made his way down the stone-footed passageways. Each of the bleak tubes of marble and pebble forked off into different directions of the unknown.

As he ventured deeper into the catacombs, Del noted varying gradients of temperature and humidity. There was no sure way he could, of course, but Del seemed to know the path he was supposed to tread. He pushed stubbornly onward.

Specters in tattered grave-cloth floated ever so subtly above the dust tracked floor, weaving their merry way. These doomed souls went about their labors, carried out as they were, deeper and deeper, into the unseen destinations of murk. They paid Del no mind. Their journey seemed pointless and dreary to Del.

A half-naked half-goat Halfling put more fuel on the fire, stoking it with a long, blackened human femur. Sparks flew up, lighting the coal black eyes of the horrid creature. It noticed Del staring. He appeared to be unsure as to where to go. The goatish Halfling briefly stopped his unending labors to point the way.

Del continued on. He traveled until he spied a long, low stone bench, large enough for a grown man. It was covered in layers and layers of filmy, filthy shroud. Yellowed and tattered, it reeked of sins done and those yet to be.

Standing next to the bench was a divine young female. She was barely dressed. Her breasts were new and perky and pointing at Del. Sweat drops dripped in steady thin streams from her dirty, dreaded hair, down her chest where they pooled at the slight upturn of her slopes.

The thickly scented perspiration then fell in pregnant raindrops to the floor where it sizzled and seethed with an almost cloying bouquet of incense. She held an ornate snuff box of priceless and ageless jewels, culled from the Dragon's belly. The lid was unclasped. Her button nose flared again and again as she spooned finely ground nose powder in rapid sequence.

Her eyes were blood red and, oh, how they blazed at Del. He was enraptured, entranced by the image of her. She held him tight with no more effort than being. She paused a moment from her spooning.

"Lie down on your belly," she told Del, "On the bench." He did. "Cover thyself with that which has been passed down from generation to generation."

Del complied in an instant, breathing in deeply the sins of the fathers. He buried his nose in the dirt and dust of ages. Lying face down, Del turned his head. Off to the side a man shouted out a warning. He slung boiling water onto the ground, spilling in a crackling wave toward the two of them. It burned everything in its path. Del's girl had her feet bare and exposed. She did not move. She smiled at Del as he looked over to her and saw how the boiling water melted the skin away. It left naught but a gray-green leathery clawed foot in its place. The herald then began to use the wet floor to strop his razor. When the straight-razor was sharp enough to slice through tin, he shaved himself complete. From top to bottom, he scraped deep and harsh. His skin tore away and he hummed with pleasure as he removed his flesh, layer by layer. The shaver stuffed the torn flesh into his mouth. He shoved, chewed, tore and swallowed the soft tissue returning from whence it came. The bloody humming man seemed happy. Hearing her sniffing again, Del returned his attention to the girl. He looked at her feet.

"Doesn't that hurt?" asked Del. He couldn't help it. Del felt protective of her.

"Of course it does," the young dread-locked girl with the melted flesh feet replied. "But pain is a form of pleasure, a precursor of it. After a time."

Del did not know how to answer that, so he said nothing. Again, he placed his face deep in the cloth. She began to massage the clenched and knotted muscles in his back. Her claws came out. Del could feel them. Her claws grew longer and sharp. They kneaded and pinched his muscles, piercing the skin, exposing the fascia, oozing and sodden.

"What are you doing to me? Del asked.

"I am helping you," she told him. "I can help you heal, Del. I can take the bad away. If you let me, that is."

"How can I do that?"

"By letting me in," she told him.

The girl rolled Del roughly over onto his back. She began to kiss him. Her ardor was filled with more hunger than passion. The girl probed Del's mouth with her tongue before shoving it, growing, down his throat. Her face followed. And then, with Del choking on her, she slid the rest of the way inside of him. Del felt whole for the first time since he shot himself. He felt great, wonderful, and he lay there for a long while. He reveled in his vigor and health. Still, he missed the girl with an ache that surprised him.

"Let me in, Del."

"Yes," he told her, "I need you." Then he awoke.

It was at that moment, when he longed for her, craving her attentions, Del awoke to what was real. Shitballs.

Oh, good fuck, he thought as he opened up his eyes. Everything was exactly the same.

You've got to be fucking kidding me.

Just when things were finally looking up, Del had to go and regain consciousness.

Damn.

EIGHT

IT WAS THE NIGHT OF LUCI AND SANCHO'S BIG PARTY at Del's house and there was a nice brisk snap to the air. The night was cloudless and filled with bright stars. The new moon slivered overhead and the sounds of merrymaking filled the sky. The music was loud, the drink was plentiful and dope was everywhere. The neighbors had already been informed, warned and threatened, depending on the individual neighbor and their asshole quotient. Del, himself, was loathed to discover that he was to be an integral part of the evening's entertainment.

There must have been close to fifty people at the gathering, all crammed together, all of them ripped out of their gourds. Del realized Sancho meant him to be there for everyone's amusement. He had rigged Del's wheelchair to go in an endless oval loop in the backyard. Del was perched in the mechanized wheelchair and strapped to the seat. Like targeting decoys in a booth at the county fair, the stoned and drunk guests were barking insults while taking turns shooting at Del with paint guns at fairly close range. Not one to limit the humiliation with Del, Sancho also had a video tape recorder set up on a tripod. It captured in glorious color Luci, coked out of her skull, blowing dude after dude in a corner of the living room. The guests would go in groups from one carnival side show attraction to the other. Sancho followed the groups, eliciting donations from whomever he could, whenever he remembered. He stuck the cash in his pocket, getting himself a nice roll. Fucked-up as he was, Sancho inevitably missed some partygoers. Those lucky bastards got to shoot the gimp or drop a nut on Luci for free. She still hadn't figured out that Sancho was using and selling her.

Or, maybe she did know, Del mused as a yellow pellet splattered his prosthetic jaw just as his chair made the turn. Maybe she gets off on the whole pimp/whore deal.

He didn't really know. But Sancho did, that's for sure. Sancho knew exactly what he was doing. Even if some freebies got past him.

Red paint struck Del full in the chest. A huge biker bellowed at the top of his voice, "Direct hit, Baby!!" He whooped and carried on, drawing to himself a crowd. When he realized all the attention he was getting, the biker strode over to Del and his endless loop. Laughing and red in the face, the biker waited until Del looped around and was coming toward him. He put his foot down in front of the wheelchair, halting its progress. "You're looking thirsty," the biker told Del. He refreshed the chair bound man by pulling out his pecker and giving Del's emaciated body a good golden shower. The big biker zipped his shit back up. Laughing hysterically, he made his way back to his buddies. High fives and pounded fists were shared, their good cheer spreading through the party crowd. No longer impeded, Del's wheelchair resumed its lonely loop.

Sancho carried a big tray everywhere he went, collecting more donations before offering the long lines of coke. It was a 'pay party' and everyone was cool with it. None of Del's old Navy buddies were invited, for obvious reasons. Del didn't think they'd be amused.

Another pellet exploded the shins of his useless legs and more strangers were yelping their pleasure and delight in Del's suffering. Everyone was having a good time.

Except for me.

"Look, the gimp's crying!" someone shouted and it was true.

Del tried his best to maintain some semblance of dignity, but the paint splashed his face and got into his eyes. The tears flowed. It was not just from the sting of the paint. It was the degradation, of course, the shame of the entire spectacle. He wanted to kill or die. Either one was fine with him.

God damn it. Those fucking assholes…

Del heard Sancho laugh derisively, adding, "And it's even the gimp's house!" This made the party goers laugh all the more.

"You're shitting me?" Del heard someone else say.

The tracks of Del's tears slinked down his paint and shame stained face. The scene worsened when it turned into an all-out convulsive crying fit. Snot ran unimpeded from Del's nose and hung off his false chin, grossing people out. People began throwing cups of beer from the keg at Del's face.

This has got to stop. Please! Help me, someone! Anyone!!

The foam mixed with the others that splashed and dripped off his face and drenched his naked, rib thin chest. Del's colostomy bag was filling from the internal pressure of his wracked sobbing fit, getting rigid and spastic. The ventilator pressure alarms sounded and kept pace with Del's despair. The continued laughter from the crowd was loud and almost comical now.

Oh Christ, oh fuck me. I'd give anything and I mean anything to –

"Get back at them?" the girl finished.

She appeared out of thin air. She sat on Del's lap, face to face with him. Her skinny arms were wrapped in an embrace around his neck and her hair was dreadlocked and smelled faintly of musk, sugar, and sulfur. She was the girl from his dream and of his dreams.

A paint pellet sailed right through her, doing no damage. Del blinked in shock. Del doubted his own eyes. The girl smiled at him.

"Oh, I am quite real," the girl assured Del, "As real as you're ever-loving soul. These bozos just can't see me, is all." Del blinked his eyes some more. The specter still straddled him. Del tried his level best to not slip out of control and go spinning headlong into madness. She added, "Aren't you getting tired of this shit?"

Yes.

"Of course you are," she replied.

What does she want from me? I don't need a massage.

"This I know."

What do you mean?

"We'll barter, you and I," she began, "just a simple exchange, for my help."

A quick splat of exploded paint pellet went through the girl's back and hit Del in his midsection, almost detaching his colostomy bag in the bargain. "You are stuck between a rock and a hard place, Delano," she told him, "And you don't really have a lot of options." Another pellet exploded, this time in the midst of Del's greasy, tangled, smelly hair. More shouts of appreciation from the crowd leaked with the paint into Del's ear. "You can let them continue to torture and humiliate you, or you can get back at them."

But, what can I do?

"By yourself, not a thing," she said, "but with my help, payback," she promised him, "will be a son of a bitch."

Del looked at the phantom. He disappointed himself for giving even a moment's credence to what she had to say. No one can help him, especially not this mirage, this little slip of a girl sitting on his lap. It was simply ridiculous.

What can she do?

"Oh my, a great deal, Delano," she told him. "Now I'm going to show you something really cool, okay? Something I think you will get a real kick out of." Del just stared at her as she spoke and the pellets whizzed in through the girl and hit him. "Now this can be a trifle startling, so you will need to steel yourself for it." She warned with a stern look on her face. "I'm going to do this so that you know without a doubt that I am serious." Del numbed and stared blankly at the girl. "You ready?" she asked.

Yes. Why not? I am already mad. I must be to entertain any of this crazy shit.

"Okay," she replied, "here goes nothing."

The girl's eyes changed first. They transformed from a deep, soulful brown to a frighteningly dark blood red. They glowed. And then her young pert face became aged and deeply wrinkled. Her face turned green like a putrid avocado. Even with his dead legs, Del could feel in an instant how heavy the creature became, perched as it was on his lap. The demon's fingers had long, dirty and yellowed nails. They were as foul smelling and as dangerous appearing as the mad jumble of gray teeth that were crowding its awful hole of a mouth.

And then, in a blink of an eye, the horrible vision turned back into the sweet looking girl. Even in his mind, Del was speechless.

"As you can see, Delano," she said, "I'm the real deal." Del stared at her. "I can make you well and help you get back at them," the girl indicated with a quick jerk of her head, the dreads bouncing.

What do I have to do?

"It's simple. All you have to do, Delano, is to invite me in," she replied with a twinkle fading from red to brown in her eyes. "But it must be a serious and formal invitation."

Saying that I do invite you in, what do you want from me in return? I know you can read my thoughts, so you know I'm not stupid or gullible.

"I know that, Delano."

There's no such thing as a free lunch.

"Also true," she agreed.

So, what is it you want from me in exchange for your help?

She smiled shyly at him. She wanted to say it out loud, but found she couldn't. Liking him, she shrugged her shoulders, instead. Then she glanced away from Del, red-faced. He didn't quite know what to make of it. But as the Texas song-bird once sang: 'Freedom's just another word for nothing left to lose'.

So, fuck it, Del thought, *I'm free. I might as well hop onboard and see where this crazy bus takes me. I sure as shit got nothing left to lose.*

NINE

THE GIMP WAS STILL PASSED OUT, SITTING IN HIS CHAIR. Sancho was watching him. He stared darkly at all the bells, whistles and doo-dads that kept the worthless fuck alive. Take the wheelchair, for instance. It was more than a chair. The big bastard was an expensive, light-weight, portable throne. Sancho figured the thing was worth more than most of the cars he'd owned. It was far too good for the likes of Sailor Del, Sancho thought. He reconnected the gimp to his breathing machine. That was another thing that Sancho thought was over-done and ridiculous. It had all kinds of knobs and dials and buttons and what-not. Del didn't need all that fancy shit to breathe. It pissed Sancho off that he didn't know enough about the machine to mess with Del more. That's why he just silenced the machine and disconnected him. Del got just as blue and his torturer had just as much fun.

Sancho knelt down on his knees. He followed Del's line and made certain that the urine catheter was knotted nice and tight. He almost wished Del didn't lay a monthly golden egg. Sancho would love to see if he could make the gimp blow up all at once, instead of dying slowly like he was.

It would be almost worth the loss of Del's government checks to do that. Not quite, but almost.

Maybe if Sancho ever won the lottery, or when he gets enough paid videotape orders for Luci's film debut (that she didn't even know about), he wouldn't need the gimp's money any longer. Once Amateur Initiations #1, starring the new adult sensation of Luci Goosey started flying off the shelves, then look out. Sancho would pay Del back, alright. He would pay the Navy fuck back in spades.

••••

AFTER DEL RATTED HIM OUT FOR DEALING, Sancho had somehow convinced himself that he would still be okay. Sancho didn't really dig being in the Navy, anyway, so it was no big hootie-doo that he was going to be tossed out on his ear. Really, who gives a rat's ass? It was all suck-ass shit work to Sancho. Taking orders and licking the boots of his superiors was not for someone as clever and resourceful as he.

In his time as a squid, Sancho experienced not one thing that would make him want to stay on after his enlistment period was up.

The Navy never stationed Sancho overseas. They taught him nothing more useful than to always keep the deck wet, in case someone important shows up. Always look busy and don't ever volunteer for anything. This was the sort of dumb shit Sancho already knew. He certainly didn't need the fucking Navy to teach him that. So, he stupidly thought his Dishonorable Discharge would be enough punishment. It was dim-witted as hell for Sancho to have thought that way. He was loathed to discover first-hand just how off base that kind of thinking was. The Navy did give him a Dishonorable Discharge, just not right away.

Sancho was tried, found guilty and sentenced to prison. The Navy waited until he served his time, and then he got his Dishonorable Discharge. He was sentenced to six years, but only had to serve three. His good behavior was enough to cut his sentence in half. Sancho didn't have much choice in the matter. When he was imprisoned, he was always too scared and abused to start much of a ruckus. Still, three years of hard time in the brig at the Naval Weapons Station was hard fucking time.

Drug dealers there are regarded slightly higher than purveyors of kiddie porn. Sancho was reminded of this almost every day. He was force-fed healthy doses of hard cock that was dished out liberally and with venom from the huge soldiers that had, maybe, a handful of functioning brain cells left between the lot of them. And those brain cells apparently told them to smack the holy shit out of Sancho.

Rusty was the ring leader. The huge craggy Lt. had criss-crossed scars all over his heavily muscled chest. He would see them whenever the unhinged Lt. would get some cohorts together and proceed to run a train on Sancho.

Rusty would call him Luci when he wanted to fuck. Sancho wasn't nearly big enough to fight back. He was a perpetual victim. His fellow prisoners regularly stole his food, which made him even weaker and more vulnerable. In fact, there were many days when semen and his own feces were all Sancho ate.

When he thought about it, he supposed he was fortunate to contract nothing more virulent than good old fashioned gonorrhea in his throat and a few busted ribs and teeth. Every night after they tired of him, Sancho would cry himself to sleep, conjuring up different ways to get back at Del.

Sancho did get Rusty, though. It was simple and ingenious. All he had to do was sprinkle some crushed glass into some raisin and rice moonshine that one of his fuck-buddies conjured up for him.

The dumb shit even scooped the bottom of his cup a few times, thinking it was un-dissolved sugar, or something. Rusty shat and vomited great gouts of blood, along with actual chunks of stomach lining. When he died, no one cared to look into it, because he was just an old, alcoholic, drug fucked, sodomizing convict. Who cares?

Sancho was released soon after. Then he saw Luci. He began talking to her and Sancho put two and two together. It made him chuckle. Luci was Rusty's kid? Aw, hell no! It was almost as if shit was planned. Add to that the tasty verity that she was also married to Popeye the fucking Sailor Man, himself.

It just can't be! Sancho remembered thinking. God must be smiling on me.

And now, as he grinned at the man passed out in his ultra-fancy wheelchair, Sancho had proof positive that god almighty existed. A total and complete reversal of fortune had occurred. His prayers had been answered. It was manifesting, right before Sancho's very eyes.

God is good. Indeed.

••••

DEL CAME TO IN HIS WHEELCHAIR and opened his eyes. He glanced down toward his lap and noticed that things were still the same. His urine catheter was still tied in a knot. The colostomy bag was an overstuffed sausage, taut as it was with Del's waste. The pressure felt from them both was nearly unbearable. The pain shot through his whole body and made him wince. At least his ventilator was attached to him. Del could hear it as it breathed evenly for him. But Del's belly was singing a different tune. It felt uncomfortably full. He looked up and saw that his feeding tube was rolled on to full. His abdomen was dangerously distended.

Del looked straight ahead. Sancho was sitting in front of Del at a card table, smiling at him.

"How you doing there, buddy?" Sancho asked Del. He was rolling a joint. A bottle of Jack Daniel's Single Barrel sat uncorked on the table. A glass of the amber liquid was splashed over rocks. Sancho's dope induced half-smile lit up his face. An IV pole stood sentinel beside him. The bag of normal saline ran through a clear tube into a plush vein on the back of Sancho's left hand. The derelict pimp drug dealer fuck had started an IV on his own self. Judging from the hooded flutter of his eyes and the way his head canted, Sancho had apparently helped himself to Del's Demerol. Sancho noticed Del staring at his IV.

"Sorry about that, Del, my man," Sancho said, licking the double wide rolling paper and twisting the ends. Sancho rolled the fat joint between his index finger and thumb to loosen the sticky, stinky bud. He took a luxurious sip of the whiskey. "I hope you don't mind that I helped myself to your pain meds." Sancho told him. "If you do mind, just say so and I'll stop," he continued with a hearty laugh. "No? Yes? What is it, then? We cool, then? Yeah, of course we are. We're friends after all, aren't we? Yes? Share and share alike, am I right?"

Del sat there motionless. He blinked rapidly at Sancho, squinting through all the pressure and pain. He hoped, so bad, that the washout fuck-tard would come closer to him. Close enough, anyway.

Come on. Pretty, please.

"I'm just gonna go and hold on to your meds, horde them, if you will," he told Del, "Since you don't mind." Del was beginning to shake from the pain and frustration. Sancho lit the joint, pulling in a deep drag. He sipped some more of the liquor. "Mmm," he added, "That god damned Demorol is delicious." Sancho scratched at his neck.

Get up, you derelict. Come on over here and fuck with me.

Sancho laughed again. But he did get up –

Yes.

– and grabbed the IV pole. He started wheeling it toward Del. "How's about some smoke, instead," Sancho offered as he approached Del's mechanical ventilator.

Sancho deactivated the pressure and volume alarms. He then took another drag off the joint, thereby keeping the cherry tip lit. He removed the adaptor from the trachea tube in Del's neck. Sancho bent at the waist and blew a thick column of cannabis down into Del's airway.

Del felt the smoke enter his virgin lungs causing them to contract and sting uncomfortably. A stir began below that and suddenly Del felt as though someone had just dumped a gallon of wet cement down his airways, filling both lungs.

Fuck, I can't breathe. I'm gonna fucking die...

"You're turning red, Del. What the matter?" asked Sancho. His grin widened with Del's discomfort. Silently, the suffering man pleaded with his torturer. Sancho ignored him. He pulled on the weed again and blew it once more down Del's throat. Del felt the cement move up from his lungs and into his trachea. Sancho stopped for a moment. Something looked strange to him. What the in the holy hell is this?

Something big...

He saw it move again.

"What the fuck?" Sancho said and he leaned in closer to get a better gander. A blood red eyeball looked back at Sancho. His own breath escaped him in a shocked rush as the eye in Del's airway hole blinked and then disappeared from view.

Something wicked...

Del was turning from red to blue as a still shocked Sancho forgot to re-connect Del to his breathing machine. Sancho was still standing flat-footed and dumb as a gray-green, ancient, wrinkled, clawed hand shot out of Del's trachea.

Here it comes...

As quick as you please, the demon grabbed Sancho's thick, luxurious hair and held it in a firm grip.

"Come on in, shit-heel," it muttered and pulled Sancho down the artificial airway and deep into Del, proper. Del took a deep, lung rattling, earth shattering breath in with a joy he'd never known. He stared at the tiny hollow IV catheter as it swung back and forth and dripped Demerol in a widening puddle on the carpeted floor.

I can breathe, I can breathe. I can fucking breathe.

And there was something else. Del could also feel his fingers and toes begin to tingle delightfully as his functions returned.

Sancho was good for something, after all.

The demon quickly leapt out of Del's neck and stood before him as the young girl.

"That was fun," she said, wiping the snot from her outfit.

The demon girl went to the card table and snatched up the JD and swigged deeply from the bottle. She then walked it and the cork over to Del, who was still sitting and breathing deliciously deep.

She grabbed hold of the airway and just yanked the fucker out. She dropped the artificial hunk of medical-grade plastic to the floor. It lay in a cradle of mucous.

The demon took the cork from the whiskey bottle and screwed it into Del's neck stoma hole.

"Have some," she said and put the bottle up to Del's plastic mouth.

He opened his new jaw for the first time. With some creaking and popping, Del took in and swallowed some. He then breathed a little more, this time through his opened mouth. He cherished the way the air felt as it passed over fuzzy teeth and a furry tongue.

The demon smiled and handed Del the bottle. He automatically reached for it with the hand that should still be dead. Del held the bottle firm and brought it to his own mouth. He hardly spilled a drop.

"Thank you," Del croaked with a voice that was weak and raspy from disuse.

He took another drink of the pricey firewater. After all, it was bought with his money.

"Try to stand," the demon girl advised.

Del was barely even shaky as he rose to a standing position. He held all of his weight on his sickly spindly fish-belly white legs. Del wobbled just a bit as he made his way slowly and carefully to the card table. He rested with his hands flat on the vinyl top and breathed some more.

"Very good," she told him, "Very good, indeed."

"Feels good," a croaking Del agreed.

"And it will get better and easier with every minute that passes," she added.

Del nodded his agreement. He noticed a plate of lined coke and a rolled, taped bill lay beside it. Del had never indulged. He was a Navy man from a long line of Navy men. He'd never tried any drugs. Del drank and swore and fucked like a sailor. He was, after all, a Navy man. Was. And so he thought, why not? Again, his money bought it. Del could hear Luci starting to stir down the hall in what used to be their bedroom. He looked over to the girl and raised his eyebrows in question.

"What do you think?" Del asked the demon.

"Why not?" she replied and slid the plate over to him.

Before he could chicken out, Del snorted up two lines, one up each nostril. He stood and sniffed. Del couldn't see what the big whoopdie-fucking-do was.

He slid it back across the table. He watched with amazement as the girl did four of the big fuckers without a twitch. And then she sat down and began chopping and lining up some more. The demon girl obviously had way more experience with blow than Del did.

"Why don't you go see Luci now," the girl advised Del. "You know, take care of some unfinished and long overdue business."

"Yeah."

"I'll come back in a little bit, give you two some privacy first."

"Yeah."

"And then," she said – chop chop chop – "we will end this."

Del looked at her. Now he was starting to feel his maiden coke rush voyage. The girl saw him looking at the coke. Without a word, she slid the plate back over to Del. He picked up the bill and snuffled up two more, much fatter, lines of cocaine.

She don't lie, she don't lie, she don't lie...

Del stood and stroked his plastic jaw.

"Yeah," he said, "Hell, yeah."

"I've got a present for you," the girl then informed Del. As soon as she said it, the gift materialized in his hand, right out of thin air.

Very cool.

"Yeah," he said once more.

Del straightened to his full height. With an invisible grin hidden beneath his man-made face, he made their way back to the bedroom. Del was going to pay Luci a visit.

Del laughed to himself as he trudged down the hall. He heard Luci's lighter clicking, getting her crack going. She was going to be surprised to see Del. He was looking forward to it. He heard her as she called out for Sancho to turn up the heat, wondering where he was. That sure made Del laugh. She's not going to believe how close the pimp piece of shit truly is.

The irony of the whole deal was scrumptious. Del couldn't wait to see his wife again. He'd help her get warm. No worries. Before long she was going to be a nicely pleasant 37 degrees Celsius and a sopping wet one hundred percent relative humidity. Soon Luci would be shown her new home. And home is a completely homeostatic bottle. One that is fit for a bitch-cunt genie like her.

It'll be all cozy, baby. You'll see.

Luci had been keeping such bad company lately and doing hard drugs all the time. She'd been letting strangers fuck her in every orifice she had to offer while Sancho filmed it.

He knew the pimp was selling it. Hell, the checks came to the house. She didn't seem to know about Sancho's enterprising little sideline. Or, if she did, she certainly didn't seem to mind being whored out like that. It was disgusting. It was humiliating and wrong.

Del couldn't wait to see his wife. He couldn't wait to straighten her bitch-ass out.

Luci had a lot of explaining to do.

Payback is going to be a son of a bitch. I shit you not.

TEN

LUCI WAS DREAMING, BUT SHE DIDN'T REALIZE IT.

In her dream she was dragged helpless down a deep, dark tunnel. She was being taken to a place that was both horrible and permanent. Luci kicked and screamed, trying her damndest to resist. She had no clue as to the where, but she did know why. It was because of Del.

It was all her fault. She allowed Sancho to torture him as he pleased; relentless and cruel. Luci never bothered to ask Sancho why he hated her husband so much, she just knew that he did. Torturing Del was almost an obsession with Sancho. She didn't know why, but as stoned as Luci always kept herself, she could tell it was something intensely personal.

In the end it didn't matter to her anyway. Del was always such a boring, wet blanket. Her husband was completely unlike her Sancho. He kept her good and high and fucked her regular and very well. The big dick bastard was so good in the sack it was almost scary. The things he did to her were amazing! Luci came so many times, her pussy almost cramped up from contracting so hard. Her cunt hurt nearly all the time. It seemed as though Sancho could come litres of spooge on her. Where did it all come from?

If she didn't know better, she might have thought that Sancho was bringing other men into bed with them. It was crazy. Sometimes, when she was really twisted, she would think he grew multiple cocks, each one fucking her in all holes and from all sides.

She vaguely recalled that happening at the big party they threw. A lot of people watched him service her with all that man-meat. Luci even imagined she was being filmed, that she was the star of a fuck-flick. There was no doubt about it, Sancho was a magic man!

She fell hard for him.

Luci grabbed at the hand that held onto her with an iron-tight grip. She'd never known Del to be like this. Rusty would have treated Luci this shamefully, she thought; but not Del. He was being so cruel. Del was roughly dragging Luci on the ground behind him. He pulled her as she was screaming, by her hair. His grip was rock solid. There was no chance of her squirming free. Still, she tried. They were making their painful, frightening way toward a solid iron door, down at the end of a long, swelling and contracting hallway. Putrid thick, charcoal colored mucous hung in globes above Luci as she was dragged by Del to the door. When they ripened fully, they dropped from the ceiling and fell on Luci. The mucous surrounded her legs. She could feel the intense pain as it enfolded her. It ate away at her flesh like acid. The door opened and a torture chamber of chains and hooks swung in merry circles. The half-dead corpses wriggled and moaned as they hung from the rusty hooks that were plunged yawning into their gray and bluing flesh. Del stopped before the Dungeon Master who stood with his immense arms folded across his chest. To Luci, the creature looked eight or ten feet tall and he smiled wicked and cruel at her. The Dungeon Master appeared to be constructed from the leftover parts that were obtained from the cutting room floor of a slaughterhouse. Blood and vile fluids dripped steadily from his mostly nude body. Nothing but a loin cloth covered his middle. His skin was rent in many places. His thick musculature was striated and visible. He had a dog's snout with an exaggerated under bite. The horns on his head were gnarled and twisting and pointing every which way. Huge multi-headed carbuncles lined his thin-haired scalp. While he was staring at Luci, getting a nice erection poking like lipstick from his sheath, he popped them. One at a time, over and over, he'd squeeze them until they squirted yellow-green arcs of filth and blood and filled the palm of his hand. Using the mess as an organic lubricant, he began to pull on himself. The fear began to build inside of Luci, fast and sure now. It grew past the pain of being pulled by her long hair. Del let go of her hair and let her drop unforgiving to the floor.

Luci pleaded, "No, Del! Please don't leave me here! Take me back up with you. I'll be good to you again, Baby! I swear!"

"Fuck off, whore," was all Del had to say.

The Dungeon Master laughed. Del held out his hand to the huge monster. Payment for goods delivered was due. The Dungeon Master dropped some gold cubits into Del's open palm.

Looking down at Luci, Del said nothing to her. No goodbyes, no fare-thee-wells. Not one word. Instead, Del sucked back a big nose glob and spat it at her. It hit solidly and splattered like thick, warm pancake batter.

Luci wiped the disgusting oyster from her face. She began to cry as Del showed her his back. He made his leave and the Dungeon Master reached down for her.

"You are fresh, my lovely," he said and quickly lifted her to her feet. He opened her mouth and stuck his foul mitt in her gob and probed her teeth. He pulled her tongue out, bending closer to enhance his inspection, before nearly ripping it out at the root. The tongue tore a bit at the base. Blood spurted out of her, crying more now. A flood of it laced down Luci's chest. The torn tongue flopped about in her mushy, dribbling mouth. Luci's cries and pleas for mercy were now met with disdain by the Dungeon Master. The huge foul hellion enforced his will with his fists. He beat her unmercifully and with glee and the greatest of delight. What fun. The Dungeon Master then mounted her. She cowed like a good subservient pit-whore should. She whimpered as he penetrated her. He fucked her with his cultivated dog cock. He moaned and pitched her profoundly; deeper and further, until she felt his dog-cock perforating something deep inside her. With growing trepidation, she looked on. Great glorious clumps of chunky blood gushed forth from between her spread legs. Scores of crying fetuses fell unimpeded from her sex, kicking and gasping for their first, last and dying breath. The miscarried babies struggled in the pool of Luci's clotting menses, trying in vain to clutch at their mother's feet, nursing futilely the tiny empty toe bones.

"Oh, no...please god help me...," Luci managed, the words barely escaping passed her blood filling, tongue flapping maw.

"You will not use his name!" the Dungeon Master howled at Luci. He pulled out of her and turned her around. He seized her by her throat, shouting, "There is no god here, Sow. You are bought and paid for. You are nothing, Trench-whore. You are my slave," he added before striking her repeatedly with both of his mammoth fists.

It was a poor, pitiful, pretty little Luci now. She was pretty no more. Hearing her jaw crack, loud and wet, was the pitiful, powerless Luci's last memory before she surrendered to the bitter darkness of her very own dreadful tale of woe. Only to awake to something much worse than just a mere bad dream….

$$\bullet\bullet\bullet\bullet$$

A BAD FEELING CROWDED HER HEART LIKE A squeezing fist. Luci was sitting straight up in bed. She was clutching the covers and bed sheets to her naked breasts. She was breathing heavily and her eyes were wide. The deep chill she'd felt when signing Rusty's paper work clenched her taut like a frozen python. Her back began to spasm. It was horrible.

Luci had woken from one fucked up dream. This surprised her in and of itself. She ate sleeping pills like candy and they all but washed away any dreams. This one felt so real and close to the surface. Even after she awoke, it was still right there with her. Luci's head hurt and her mouth was desert dry. A bottle of sports drink – the cokehead's favorite form of nourishment – sat on the night stand. She reached for it, twisting off the top and chugging most of it down. She belched and used the sheet to wipe her mouth. The dream was fading fast. Good. But the cold spasms remained.

Run, Luci!

Luci picked up her glass pipe and loaded a rock in the end. She clicked the lighter and touched the pipe with flame.

Luci pulled in the thin wisps of smoke. She leaned back against the headboard and held it in. She stretched long, releasing the built up tension in her neck and back. She wondered where Sancho was. It's cold in here.

Save yourself! He's coming!

Luci called out for Sancho to turn up the fucking heat, but he didn't answer. And then, as surreal as her realistically rotten nightmare had been, she saw him. Del stood in the doorway.

"Hi honey," Del told Luci. "Look what the cat dragged in."

ELEVEN

THE DEMON GIRL SAT AT THE TABLE. She was snuffling up Sancho's cocaine like a Hoover. The rush was peaking like a freight train off its rails. She started bouncing her heel off the carpet and humming sweet and gentle nonsense. She sniffed deep into her sinuses, treasuring the drip that was draining down the back of her throat. Her esophagus recoiled as the tissue swelling made it feel as though something was stuck down there. She did another line anyway. The demon girl put her head back and gently shook it from side to side, coaxing the cocaine to soak into her mucosa. This was getting fun. In various forms and incarnations throughout the millennia, the ancient demon had dallied with humans, whenever he grew weary of his own kind. The Damned were so fucking boring. They were always bitching and bemoaning their eternal plight. Languishing in their own despair those fools failed to realize that Satan has dominion over the Earth and its creatures. It takes a great deal of concentration and effort to consort on terra firma, and few of them ever tried. It was simply too much god damned work for them. It was much easier to wait for the damned to arrive and fuck with them then instead.

Boring!

THE PLACE IN BETWEEN

Fuck that lame-ass shit. Those lazy bastards could have them. It was about as challenging messing with the new arrivals as it was to force-fuck a nymphomaniac with her knees pinned by her ears. Where's the test in that?

Fortunately for said demon, sightings and possessions were rare enough to be considered mere myths and he was certainly glad of that. It allowed him to move about the planet freely. Even so, it took him centuries of human time to become adept at playing with the Bright White Father's favorite creations.

There were, naturally, certain rules one must follow to avoid complications and confrontations with those strong enough to shit in the demon's bowl of mead. After a few early and unfortunate encounters, the demon learned why the rules were the rules. They were written for a reason; you get your pee-pee slapped hard if you break them. It's just not worth the irritation.

Since then, the demon always sought to fly 50 feet below the radar, as Del's Navy friends liked to say. It was very sound advice.

The basic principle went something like this; unless you were given irrefutable permission from Upstairs, the pious were absolutely off-limits. Those that follow Downstairs are protected under the Dark Wing and can only be played with their own personally granted permission.

That's no fun at all. However – and this was what the demon lived for – all others that were on the spiritual sidelines were considered fair game. And this visage of a young girl; man, it was such a hoot. The demon couldn't wait to see where it took him.

She heard Del laugh and Luci scream. The demon girl bent to the plate and did just one more big, fat rail of blow. Then she rose with a smile and walked on down the hall. It was time for her to join the program.

Apparently, it was already in progress.

TWELVE

I'M SORRY, BABY.

Del came into the bedroom. He was wearing nothing but the filthy cotton house pants that Sancho and Luci kept him in. His head was full of coke and hate and his heart was full of pain. He stared at the woman who was staring right back at him with her mouth open in shock. He hated her so much. Mostly it was because he had loved her so much. His right hand held the demon's gift. Del hid it behind his back.

"Where's Sancho?" Luci asked, pulling the bedding up to cover her shameful nakedness.

Del could not believe it. There was no how are you standing, or I'm sorry, just where's Sancho?

"You don't need to concern yourself with that derelict piece of pimp shit," Del told her as he entered the bedroom. She cringed up against the headboard. "He's nearby."

"Is he okay?" Luci asked with concern. "Is he hurt? Did you hurt him, Del?"

Del considered that. "Good question," he told her.
I don't know. Not really. He isn't moving around much, though.

"What did you do to him?" she asked and, "How are you able to walk?"

Finally!

"You should really start worrying more about what I'm going to do to you, to answer your first question," Del replied. "As to your next question, never you fucking mind, you skanky whore."

Luci's jaw dropped open when Del showed her the demon's gift. He put the target loaded .45 to her temple. With his free hand Del pulled Luci off the bed by her hair. She landed on the floor with a satisfying thud.

"Ow, Del," Luci cried out. "Stop it, you're hurting me."

"If you like that, just you wait, honey," Del promised her. "I'm just getting warmed up. I can't wait for you see what I've got planned. You're going to get a real kick out of it, Doll."

Del tugged his knotted urine catheter out of his penis. His bloated over loaded bladder released in a pressured spray of urine, blood and infection all over the front of Luci. She began to cry.

"I want you to remove my shit bag," he ordered. When Luci did not comply with Del's wishes fast enough, he wiped the disgusted look off her face. Del smacked her a good one, using his heavy gun hand for emphasis. The blood that ran thick from her face made sure Luci had gotten the message. Still crying, but complying, Luci removed the colostomy bag from Del's bloated belly. Shit splattered Del's midsection as the back-up became unplugged. The smell was offensive. "Now douse yourself with it." She looked to her husband with horror. Del pressed the gun into her eye socket. He wasn't kidding around. "Do it," he said.

Luci took the full bag and anointed her crown with the foul perfume. The satanic baptism ran into her eyes, nose and her mouth. It made her projectile vomit the contents of her stomach. Much of the sports drink drenched Del's middle.

Del laughed uproariously and Luci screamed in disgust.

•••
_____

RUSTY WAS HANGING ON LUCI'S BACK. The ghost knew his step-daughter was in more trouble than she knew. If Luci thought it was bad enough what Del was doing to her, just wait until that dreadlocked little bitch comes in. Then the whole house of cards was going to crumble.

Oh, fuck, here she comes.

The demon came into the bedroom. She was sniffing back the coke and she was smiling, pleased. Del noticed her, but Luci didn't. She was too far gone now to care. Her tears were mixing with the feces and vomit that covered her like a confirmation gown. The curdled, multi-hued mess ran lava-slow until it curled around Luci's knees. The demon girl smiled grandly at Luci's speedy capitulation.

Maybe, if I plead with her.

The demon saw the ghost that had Luci wrapped in a death-grip. Now that's interesting, She thought. Not a problem, but worth noting. The demon hadn't seen Rusty since Vietnam, almost twenty years ago.

"You know you can't stop us," the demon told the specter.

Leave her be, Sir. Please, Sir.

"No," she replied.

Please? It wasn't supposed to be like this. You never said it would come back to haunt her. She didn't bargain with you, Sir, I did.

The girl just shrugged her shoulders to that. It's not her fault if Rusty didn't read the fine print.

Please, Sir, just leave her be!

"There will be SILENCE!" she commanded and Rusty complied. He had no choice. It was orders from a superior officer. There was nothing he could do. He wasn't leaving Luci alone though. Rusty was certain of that.

He'd bide his time, make himself small and wait for an opening.

• • • •

DEL WAS LESS SURE OF HIMSELF NOW. He'd watched the exchange between them. Del thought he saw the demon girl talking to Luci, but what she said didn't make any sense to him. What couldn't be stopped? Who needed to be silent? It was bewildering.

Del visibly deflated. He wasn't completely well yet and he appeared to be plagued with self-doubts. The poor guy came across as much more pensive and hesitant than the demon girl knew Del to be.

Sadly, she could tell that he still clung to shreds of feelings for the whore. It made the demon want to obliterate Luci himself with his bare, clawed hands. But the demon knew that jealousy was a caveat of love, so he let the feeling pass. She glanced up at Del instead.

"What now?" he asked her. Del clearly needed some help in decision making. The demon's grin spread and her eyes turned red again.

"Let's reunite the lovebirds," she suggested.

Careful to avoid all of the filth, the demon girl skirted the decrepit puddle and took the few strides from Del's side and got up onto the bed. She began jumping up and down like a little kid. Del watched her happily.

"Are you ready?" she asked. Del nodded while Luci still cried and carried on. "Here we go!" she sang with glee. The demon leaped up high in the air. Del had his head back. He popped the cork out and braced himself. With a *wheeee* the demon girl flew through the air and dove right down Del's neck hole.

Del replaced the cork in his neck. He straightened out his head and looked down at his wife. He used the serious end of the .45 to lift her chin to him. Luci opened her beautiful blue eyes and gazed with trepidation at her husband. She blubbered and her rough hitching breaths sounded painful.

"No," she begged. "Please, Del!"

"Yes," he told her, "You're next." Del would have smiled if he could. He ran a finger around the inner rim of his naked colostomy. "But this is how you are getting in, buttercup," Del explained to a paling and shivering Luci. "You're going in through the out door."

Luci did not want to, but she did comply. Luci entered Del's stoma with a taut balloon pop. Del watched as her feet disappeared inside of him. The cold Luci felt was finally gone. Del screwed another liquor bottle cork into place, trapping the genie in its bottle for all time.

Sorry Luci. Sorry for everything. Rusty sat his ghost-ass in the corner of the bedroom and cried and cried.

THIRTEEN

THE EXAM ROOM AT THE EMERALD CLINIC of the Veterans' hospital smelled of fresh paint and strong disinfectant. Del was sitting on an exam table while the wound care nurse removed his colostomy bag for the last time. She cleaned the stoma, preparing to let it heal and close shut.

"Just keep it clean and dry and it should close on its own in a few days," she told Del.

Del's recovery had been nothing short of miraculous. Not only could he walk and breathe on his own, he even regained full use of his gastrointestinal tract. The hole in his neck had closed on his own. Del was putting on weight and feeling great. He just had to be careful of the little things that could still manage to trip his shit up. Like when he unknowingly pooped out something that was too solid to digest fully. Del had to make sure he cleaned out his colostomy bag before coming in today to see the wound care nurse. It would be kind of hard to explain to her if she was to find a bit of finger bone, or toe.

Del was happy he was finally free of the shit bag. Digging through it was disgusting. But sometimes it yielded interesting mementos. He had fished out Luci's gold wedding band and her diamond engagement ring a little while back.

Luci wanted the rings back, but Del felt they were no longer married to each other. Not in the eyes of god. The rings were simply returned to their rightful owner, Del. He could do with them whatever he wished.

Luci herself was still in residence inside Del. Sancho had been still from the beginning, but Luci kicked up a fuss whenever she could manage it. Going to the clinic at the VA, that was kind of nerve wracking. And Del knew it was Luci's doing when the nurse paled. She was looking closely at the colostomy, making sure it was clean and dry enough to close on its own. That's when she saw what she could have sworn was a beautiful blue eye winking at her from deep inside Del's open stoma.

The nurse felt so poorly, she had to struggle to keep from passing out on the floor in front of Del. He helped her sit. He stuck his head through a crack in the door and called for some assistance. When help arrived, they didn't understand what had happened. The nurse refused to say anything and Del refused to be re-examined. He was fine. "Just look after your fallen comrade, why don't ya," he told them. "I feel good, I'm fine."

Shit, Del felt right as rain. In fact, he felt great.

They stared at Del's back as he hummed his happy way out of the hospital and out to the parking lot.

"What the hell happened?" the doctor asked the nurse. She just sat there, paling, refusing to say any more on the matter. From the window, the doctor stared at Del as he walked to his handicap parking spot. He appeared to be talking to his belly; chastising it, in fact.

"Wow," the doctor replied, genuinely surprised. "Now that was different." The staff all laughed. It was a good tension breaker. The wound nurse didn't laugh, however. She still felt like hammered shit. She wasn't looking so hot, either. No one was surprised when the nurse finally fainted.

Del got into his pick-up truck and started the engine. Luci was still trying to get out through Del's tightening colostomy. He was driving the vehicle home when he noticed partially digested finger bones. The bones poked out of the remaining shredded flesh of Luci's fingertips. The tips had been eaten away from the acid in Del's gastro-intestinal system.

"Let me out, Del," Luci begged. Her fingers were replaced with teeth. She was trying to force them out. Her lipless mouth was pressed up against the hole in his belly, trying her fair-weather best to force herself out of Del's stoma. She was attempting to get in some fresh air and plead with Del at the same time. Neither was working very well. "Please, baby," she continued, "I'll be good this time, I swear."

"Shut the fuck up, you slut whore," Del responded, "You've already been replaced." Then he slammed a hammer fist down into his own sore belly, effectively ensuring Luci's silence, at least in the short term.

As Del drove slowly home, he reflected. It was strange, for sure, this turn of events. Essentially, Del was in love with a denizen of Hell. Too fucking weird. It made him chuckle. He didn't care. He'd given all his heart to Luci and she fucked him over for a worthless derelict, so fuck her. Del was never really that spiritual. It wasn't that he didn't believe in god or the devil, he just didn't give a shit. He never really thought that much about it. But now he did. Del knew his returned health was nothing short of a miracle and that this said miracle was provided by a demon because this devil had never experienced love before. Not in all the countless ages had he. But Del and his hideous plastic prosthetic jaw-piece was the object of this demon's desires. That was hunky-dory to Del. Even if he would have to spend an eternity in the fiery pit, he felt it was worth it. After all, where the fuck was god almighty when Luci was sucking strange cock and Sancho was disconnecting him from his life support? Huh? Well?¡ Just where the fuck was he then? Where was god when Del needed him most? Del didn't know. Hell, no one knows, so fuck it and fuck him. Del would happily take his chances with the dark side. Honestly, what Del felt he deserved right down to his toes is that he should be let go for time served. Maybe he deserved the torture and humiliation for committing a mortal sin, or maybe the punishment was too harsh. He didn't know. Either way, Del would be quite satisfied with a no harm, no foul frame of mind. Fuck it. Who cares anymore? Del was just so glad to be content again. Let the chips fall where they may.

Del made it home. He pulled into the lot and parked his car. Del came up the walk to his place. He unlocked the door and let himself in. Del dropped his keys on a table and went into the living room. As he looked fondly around the place, as he always stopped to do these days, he marveled at how well he was able to remove every scrap and trace of Sancho and Luci's presence.

Del had had himself a great, big, old fashioned barbeque clothes burning party. He got rid of everything of theirs. It was almost like they were never there. Not many people asked, but to those that were curious Del simply said the two lovebirds ran away together. They were not heard from again.

Del turned around and went into the kitchen. He was thirsty enough for a beer or three while setting up the grill. He opened up the refrigerator, marveling at food actually being in the ice-box. Del reached for the platter of pineapple and tequila soaked shrimp. Balancing the plate with one hand, Del grabbed a beer with the other. He opened it up, slugging the frosty brew back on the way out to the porch.

Once there, he placed the plate on a table. He snatched up a box of long-tipped matches and went to the nearby grill. Del poured charcoal briquettes into a bowl over the ashes of previous barbeques and fired up the cone. While the flames were licking the sky, Del turned on a small television, tuning in to March Madness. He was enjoying the light spring chill, listening to some college hoops as pleasant background noise. He sighed with deep satisfaction and sweetly lingering delight.

Del was realistic. He knew the Navy would never let him back in with his medical issues. They were also not entirely convinced that his injuries were sustained as an accidental discharge during routine cleaning. Del didn't put up any fuss. He knew how fortunate he was, more so than them. His monthly Social Security and Disability checks more than covered his nut. Sancho and Luci were never sober enough to locate his investments. Del was still financially solvent. Even the house they were in was rented in Del's name. There wasn't even a need for him to move. Del's old Navy friends began coming around to see him. They were getting more and more comfortable with Del's new plastic face. And they just loved Luci's absence. She was such a cunt.

This new one of Del's seemed awfully young to them. Too young for Del, for sure, but it was even more than that. The girl looked too fucking young, his friends thought, for anyone that wasn't still squeezing whiteheads and jerking off to yearbook pictures of cheerleaders. Some of his buddies even suspected that she might be underage. It was hard to tell, though. Some people just looked young. Still, Del seemed quite happy with her and lord knows Del deserved it. He never talked about his illness and Del never discussed Luci, her boy toy, or her myriad indiscretions. They didn't know. They were happy for him and his obvious happiness. So much so they all decided, individually as well as collectively, to leave well enough alone. Eventually this new one would turn eighteen. Sooner rather than later, they fervently hoped.

Del's own opinion on the matter was that all in all things turned out alright. And as the demon girl came sniffing red-nosed outside to the back porch and wrapped her skinny arms around Del's middle, he thought, maybe even better than alright.

The demon girl brought out a little tooter and placed it under Del's nose. He snorted the coke and then he hit the other side. The grill was ready. The shrimp sizzled just like the Roman steam bath in the dream he had during one of his many Sancho torture sessions. The smell was enticing and his girl massaged Del's bunched, sore muscles with delightful enchantments. It was as intimate as Del and the girl ever got. Sancho and Luci and all the vile sex bullshit he was forced to witness ruined him for all time when it came to the act of love. They snuggled and smooched and that was about it.

"Give me some of your blow, Del," a muffled Luci begged from deep within. "Please, Papi. Please?"

"You can stow that shit, right now, fuck-slut," Del answered, then sucker-punched his own belly again. He heard something crack and detach from Luci. She was either knocked out, or contrite enough to be quiet, following the strike. Anyway, he couldn't care less. Just as long as she shut the fuck up. Del was getting weary of her. He looked to his girl. He asked her, "How much longer do I have to listen to this shit?"

"Not much longer, Daddy," she replied, giving his nose another taste of cola. "You'll crap out her bones, soon enough," she promised. Del nodded. He thought that would be fine. He'd absorbed all of Sancho, seemingly in an instant. The pimp piece of shit gave it up so sweet; perhaps he should be given the nickname Azucar. With Del's stubborn wife and her strong will to live, it would apparently take a little while longer. No problem. As he glanced at the ancient demon beside him, all gussied up in his girlish finery, Del knew he came out on top.

The demon looked up at him lovingly. She smiled. Del took her hands in his, kissing them. Luci's engagement and wedding rings looked real nice on her delicate little fingers. It was the first time she'd ever been in love.

And it was something fierce.

Meanwhile, the ghost of Rusty eyed the two of them. He watched them closely. Hanging on in quiet desperation is the limbo way. They were lovers entwined, kissing and smiling at one another. If the Lt. had a working stomach, it would have turned over. It was gross what they were doing. Periodically, the façade of the school girl slipped away and the foul demon residing beneath the mask peaked out. Rusty noticed that Del's eyes were always closed when this happened. He couldn't bear to watch, so he decided not to.

Those sick fucks!

Rusty turned on his heels, leaving the way he came. He floated back to the bedroom. There he sat killing time. Rusty waited behind the tiny dust bunny in the corner of the bedroom. Rusty was just aching for the opportunity to free Luci from Del's anatomic prison. Freeing her would have to earn him forgiveness. Then Rusty would take the both of them home. He knew he could do it. Rusty just had to get to Del when the demon girl was away.

Finally, the opportunity arose for him to try an attempt at rescuing Luci. After climbing the bed, Rusty made his ghostly way over to a slumbering Del and his closed belly stoma. He forced his hands into Del's stoma, opening it up wide enough for Rusty to slip inside. Finally, he was here. Now all he had to do was locate her.

Luci, baby….where are you?

Rusty stood inside of Del, in his sludgy colon. Using his ghost-eyes, he began trudging along, looking and calling out for Luci. He was bound and determined to find her and save her.

No matter how long this final mission might take. Rusty would keep looking. Time ceased to have any meaning for him. He found it more than a little curious that he found himself back in the shit. Rusty could search for Luci until the end of all came. Then the forces of good, and that which has been tainted as evil, would come calling to claim them.

Even if he couldn't find her at all he would keep searching. Even if she had already been completely and irretrievably absorbed by Del, he wouldn't give up. Even if all Rusty found waiting for him inside of Del was nothing more than a big old pile of Luci's bones.

Even if all of that was so, Rusty wouldn't ever quit trying to save Luci. He had to continue his relentless quest for her. This was his penance. To spend an eternity seeking out that which had been lost; that was the price he must pay. To be denied both salvation and damnation. To be stuck forever in the place in between. This is forevermore for Rusty.

THE PLACE IN BETWEEN

There was no one left to miss him. There would be no-one lighting candles and beseeching the saints to save Rusty's immortal soul. He would never find the one he sought so diligently. Rusty would be doomed to search for Luci forever. And when that forever was finally finished, only the damned would remain to welcome him home. There would be nothing else left.

Rusty never noticed the dread-locked girl as she was falling in lock-step, right behind him. She was following him, goose-stepping down Del's colon. Even when she caught up to Rusty and reached out for him, he didn't see her.

Unfinished business.

"A bad beginning makes a bad ending."

–EURIPIDES

IN–COUNTRY, 1968

THE TET OFFENSIVE WAS THE REAL GENESIS. For Rusty, it all went to hell right after Tet. That's when the drinking and drugging took center stage. Heroin and Jack Daniels, Mamma-san; that was Rusty's cocktail of choice from Tet on. Charlie Company supplied the Tennessee sipping whiskey and the gook whores provided the smack. Project 100,000 endowed Rusty with the government sanctioned psychopaths he needed to complete his missions. Criminals, social deviants and the magnificently deranged fell then under the lieutenant's command. Rusty scooped up his favorite sergeant, Del's father. The heroin, the whiskey and the blood lust took care of the rest. He was in this frame of mind when he and his gaggle of killers got their marching orders. It was time for reprisal against the VC. The Viet Cong had some pay-back coming.

Lieutenant's Rusty had a 0–dark–30 mission start time. It was still hours before he and his men's scheduled combat drop behind lines and he needed to get his head right. Perched up on a big chair in a shabby hut in a nondescript, friendly village, Rusty was getting his dick sucked. The boy doing it had the fluttering eyes and general slovenly demeanor of a heroin addict. The boy's Mamma-san was using some hosiery to tie off the lieutenant. She had a loaded syringe of top grade Dragon's Breath direct from the Golden Triangle. Rusty liked to use opium wrapped in joint-rolling paper to dissolve slowly in his rectum when he was in the jungle and deep in the shit. But before he started a mission, Rusty always ran a big load in his veins. Mamma-san shot him up, loosening the hose and letting it hit Rusty with full force. The euphoric rush felt like it lifted Rusty from the ground. He'd lost his line of sight. Finally, he came down enough to realize just what he'd done. The lieutenant apologized to the screaming woman. He didn't know he had killed the boy that was servicing his cock until he had awoken with the boy's decapitated head staring back at him.

Sorry about that. The devil made me do it.

The lieutenant's mission was a resounding success. Rusty wasn't the only officer involved, though he was by far the most victorious. The twin tragedies of My Lai and Co Luy were well suited to showcase Rusty's ruthlessness. He and his sergeant became the Army's de-facto, go-to guys. It enhanced Rusty's position and solidified the officer's resolve. He took comfort in knowing that some of those in charge actually wanted to win this pariah of a war.

Rusty was still deep in the shit when the orders came through to scoop him up. He had killed, depending on accounts, anywhere from 200 to 500 civilians. He probably could have gotten away with it if he hadn't insisted on the kills being classified as confirmed. Fuck, man. Rusty was just following orders. For My Lai and Co Luy, he really was following orders from on high. Since he was on the ground and the orders came from far away, Rusty got left holding the bag for his superiors.

The drink, the drugs and the thugs got him started on the path that led inexorably to Pinkville, the shameful stain and beyond. You can't blame it all on the pieces that make up the complex puzzle. It is the hard heart that kills. It is the unblinking eye that holds the target in place. It is the steady trigger-finger that does not hesitate at the moment of truth. It is the hard heart that kills.

Rusty and the sergeant had that to spare. And they had a hell of a lot of work left to do.

•   •   •   •
═══

RUSTY, THE SERGEANT AND THEIR MERRY BAND of cut-throat killers herded a group of twenty villagers and corralled them together. They had already burned their huts to the ground and slaughtered the livestock. They had no vehicles and no weapons to speak of. Still they were Viet Cong, unless proven otherwise. The group was crying and pleading and carrying on so much the unrelenting noise was slicing right through the heroin and whiskey. It was giving Rusty a bad tension headache. And that little problem was something Rusty could fix. He would just have to shut them up. Ordering them to strip their clothing off at bayonet point, they separated the women to one side. Taking turns, Rusty and his men raped and sodomized every single one, from the steel-gray grandmothers on down to the smallest of crawlers. Rusty, smacked out of his cranium on horse and liquored to the gills, led the charge into the fray. He went all gray and cloudy inside. He was fevered and speaking in tongues. Rusty took his knife from its sheath and began cutting his chest in a grotesquely rhythmic fashion. It helped to fuel his rage garnered erection.

Even for him, Rusty was getting way out of bounds. Even the killers in his squad were taken aback. Rusty's ferocity knew no limits. It could not be contained. A tiny, dread-headed girl sat on the cartilage of Rusty's ear and spoke to him. She encouraged him in his ruthless pursuits. One of his men snuck away with a field phone to attempt to call in the crime as it was happening. The sergeant noticed the soldier ducking for cover and preparing to run away. He told Rusty who listened and dismounted, leaving the girl he was molesting to die alone in a pool of her wasted life. Bleeding from the self-inflicted knife wounds and covered in the filth and blood of his victims, Rusty strolled purposefully toward the discontented.

Get him.

"You fuck, or you die," the lieutenant told his man, without preamble. The boy said naught. "You fuck, or you die," repeated Rusty.

The soldier turned to run.

Get him!

Letting out a battle howl, Rusty charged after the runaway and gave chase. This was perfect. The chase allowed Rusty's heart to pound and his already hot blood to boil. The kid was running flat out, balancing an army field telephone and un-holstering his sidearm. The soldier was glancing fearfully over his shoulder as he heard Rusty pounding the jungle floor in hot pursuit. The kid was attempting to crank the phone while running flat-out, and scared out of his mind. It was no small feat. The soldier was just getting a connection, when Rusty finally caught up to him. They were deep in the jungle. The canopy here was so thick, only shadows and pencil thin shafts of muted light made it to the spongy earth. The lieutenant clenched the struggling, frightened soldier by his hair and spun him around.

Gut him, Princess. Gut him like a pretty little fishy.

THE PLACE IN BETWEEN

The kid tried to bring up his gun and Rusty gutted the boy like a catfish. The boy seemed too surprised to be holding a handful of his own guts. Rusty retrieved a mess of the boy's inners and shoved them deep into the dying soldier's mouth. He let the boy fall to the jungle floor, a long strand of intestine quivered in his grip as the boy fell. He let go of the boy's guts and grabbed his tags.

Standing now with a handful of wet, warm bowel, Rusty looked down to his blood-drenched hands for a moment. Then he reached up and, with his hands, Rusty smeared the dead kid's blood all over himself. Just as quickly as it happened, Rusty forgot about killing one of his own men. In his mind, the soldier died in the line of duty.

Rusty made his way back to the unholy skirmish. When he got there he told his men, "Kill one man, the right man, and you can terrorize a thousand." He tossed the sergeant the dead soldier's dog tags. He looked into their staring, startled faces. Then they all agreed vocally with their lieutenant's sentiment. As any man would when your boss is wiping some of your colleague's blood on his pants while smiling such a ruthless and satanic smile.

This motherfucker is truly unhinged, they thought, killing one of their own. That's not right. And speaking of not right, what was it with Rusty anyway? Why did the lieutenant make them fuck the wrinkled ones? Fucking sick, that's what it is.

After the ferocious festival of fun was over, they herded all the gooks still breathing into a ditch.

"What do we do with them, Sir?"

Rusty looked at his sergeant and said, "You know full well our standing orders, sergeant. We shoot anything that moves. Don't ever forget. It will save your life someday." Rusty's goons mowed them all down with machine gun fire. They left none standing. As they were walking away, Rusty's sergeant asked him how they should report the incident.

"Hell, we only suffered one casualty," he said. "What do you think? I call that victory." Rusty wiped his blade clean on the bright green ground and smiled. "Besides, if it's Vietnamese and it's dead, well shit, it's VC. We got twenty confirmed kills, Sarge." Rusty plastered his best thousand-watt smile on his gore-stained face. "Call it in."

Del's father did exactly that.

The tiny dancer in Rusty's ear watched these atrocities with glee from the vantage point of her front row seat. He never disappointed her. He could always be counted on to deliver the goods.

Lieutenant Rusty was a preferred customer.

"One loyal friend is worth ten thousand relatives."

-EURIPIDES

STATESIDE, 1962

EVERYONE KNOWS THAT THE SHIT ROLLS DOWNHILL. Year after year and generation upon generation it does. Sins of the fathers, you know. Sins of the fathers cannot ever be forgotten and they cannot be forgiven. No one can escape gravity. No matter how hard we try. Round and round and round it goes.

Where it stops, nobody knows.

••••

SERGEANT RUSTY WAS SITTING ON A BARSTOOL when the young-looking girl came into the tavern. He had just been denied Officer Candidate School for the second time. His psych evals were lacking the necessary bottom to lead, they had told him. His conduct was also considered unbecoming. Rusty was nursing his beer and brooding into his shots of Jack. He had just the one last chance of getting into OCS before he would have to decide on remaining in the Army as an enlisted man or just get out.

There was a war ramping up in Southeast Asia and he didn't want to get out of the Army. Rusty wasn't good at anything other than being a soldier. He felt he belonged there. It was all he knew. Rusty knew he'd make a fine officer if the tight-asses would just give him a chance.

"Why so glum, chum?" the girl asked him as she plopped on the barstool next to him. Rusty turned to look at her. She was adorable with her soulful brown eyes and crazy dread locked hair. Rusty didn't think he wanted to talk, but there was something about her that made him open up.

"My career is tanking, and there's not a God-damned thing I can do about it," he divulged. "So I think you and I should sit right here and help me drown my sorrows. What do you say?"

"Sure," she said. The bartender brought them both another round of the same and they tucked right in. They chinked their shot glasses in a toast to his dubious future. The girl was trying to convince Rusty to not give up on OCS. "I can help you," she told him. Rusty didn't believe a word she was saying to him. Plus she gave him a bad feeling, like his heart was being crushed in a coldly frigid vice-grip. The pain in his chest was uncomfortable, but he couldn't stop looking at her. She told Rusty that he should take her home. She was inviting him in. Rusty thought he might just do it. He was randy as all get-out and she sure was cute. She was jail-bait, though. He could tell. Rusty eyed her critically.

"How old are you, anyway," Rusty asked her. She smiled.

"Don't worry, I'm much older than I look," she assured him. Then she tossed another shot of whiskey back, slammed the empty glass on the bar and laughed uproariously. "Besides you look like someone in desperate need of a good friend. Am I right?" she asked, still laughing. Rusty joined in, starting to feel real good. She was right. Rusty did want of a friend, a loyal one, and he needed it in the worst way.

Regardless…

In the end, it was the heavy throb of what she must look like naked that sealed the deal. Oh, yeah, that and her eyes. They were magnetic, drawing him in, like a moth to a flame. He found them irresistible.

Rusty just loved the way her eyes turned red when she laughed.

….END

Morbidbooks Is A Grotesque Bizarro Ballet Where The Most Profane Things Occur. An Impious And Perverse Dwelling Of Dark Revulsion. A Cozy Cottage Where Torture Porn And Brutal Bible Tales Are Devised. A Quiet Place To Relax And Spin Tales Of Depravity And Wickedness. A Halfway House For The Disturbed Where Rules No Longer Apply. A Safe Haven For Deviant Serial Killers To Hatch Their Wretched Schemes. Bring Your Pets. The Tasty Ones Are Always Welcome.

HTTPS://WWW.MORBIDBOOKS.WORDPRESS.COM

~ **It wasn't long before the contents of his mysterious** trunk were revealed to her. It was true, they were props, and some of them might even have been used in the circus. Whips and crops, handcuffs, gags and blindfolds. He applied each of them to her liberally and with sadistic abandon. She took to each of them and craved more. This was the other side of Salero, the one he hid, the dark side. Publically, the man loved and craved the laughter and applause of children. But as much as he craved the laughter of children, he also craved the cries and screams of women as they submitted to his own particular brand of sadism. He wielded a whip better than any lion tamer in the business. It thrilled him to watch the firm young flesh of a woman writhe and twist in delicious agony as his ropes bit deeply into them and his crops left myriads of latticework markings on their bodies. Their anguish was his delight.

~**Rae is her name.** Our support group of embittered and most likely deranged women are going to kidnap, torture, disembowel and finally kill the woman who has ruined all our lives. As foul and as grotesque as she is, she acts like she's Queen of the Bean. Rae, her buck-tooth grin and rosy cheeks of middle age acne reflected winter sun. Straw-like blonde hair obscured by the veil and tiara she enjoyed parading around in. She walked past our window with sickening confidence oblivious to us and our weak tea. Rae. Everything was always about Rae. Was she a princess today, or was she a bride? We wished we could be that delusional and walk around with an air of not giving a damn. Rae believes she is above the pain she has caused. Beyond the whimpering of her victims. Out of reach of vengeance. Our support group of women do not agree. Judgement day is here for Rae.

~Maybe it had started when he was at university.

He had a girlfriend in his final year that had gotten him into some weird stuff sexually then she left him for a guy with a bigger cock. The other guy was some gay looking chump with muscles and a tattoo; the pair had died in a car accident and Brian took a dump on their graves after each of their funerals. Fuck the both of them. But after she had left him he needed to fill the void of the newfound enjoyment of sickening sexual practices. Brain had purchased one of those 'real life' sex dolls online. Boy did the thing look real; you could bend it into any position and it came armed with enormous tits, willing mouth and a supposedly real feel pussy and anus. The packaging said to 'just add lubricant' but there was a problem. There was something missing; the smells, the tastes and the feel of real skin. You can't emulate that. So Brian set out to attempt to build a real life sex toy made from real life people.

~I ORDER A magic lamp from the internet. According to the seller, it is good as new, and after rubbing the thing, a djinn will come out and give me three wishes. I begin to rub the lamp. Along with some dark smoke a thin, bald guy crawls out. His skin is all grey, the eyes are colorless pebbles.

"I want a tree which grows money as leaves!" I command.

"I never realized life can be so short. We are just putting the bricks, one into another, and then we try to climb over the wall that we created. But it is so big. It covers the sun." he mutters.

"I want a sports car!" I try again, but he just looks out in the window, gazing the clouds, telling me: "Can cancer grow in birds? Does it kill owls in the forest, or eagles in the mountains? The deer maybe? The giant fish on the bottom of the sea?"

With a desperate look I say: "I want a swimming pool."

But the djinn begins to cough up blood, and it is damned sure, I won't get any swimming pool today.

~**Keegan is a late-night public access radio show host,** sexual deviant, and militant vegan. He has grown tired of his vegan cause being treated with apathy by the portly, meat-gorging, residents of the small town of Breen Gay, Wisconsin.

The time is ripe for Vegan vengeance.

Keegan harvests roundworms from a local vagrant and mutates them using chemicals stolen from the meat packing plant. He infests the populace with the voracious, parasitic carnivores. Keegan knows that the only way for the people of Breen Gay to eliminate the parasites is to starve them of meat.

It is with great expectation that he awaits the oncoming utopia of Veganism.

However, the mutant roundworms will not die easily. The problems for the people of Breen Gay have only just begun.

~For so long as anyone could remember, The Flagrant Five
have ruled the land with an aggressive hand—enslaving
children, destroying the wilderness—but Father Necrocious is
tired of it all. One of his worst enemies (and a member of the
Flagrant Five), Manservant Genesis, has escaped his
imprisonment as a shadow.Therefore, he's enlisted the help of
a ragtag group of fabricated Mercenaries to turn the fascists
to shadows. The annual Dictators' Ball is pending (a battle in
which children are used as pawns to determine the fate of the
free world), and the brothers plan to stop the gala before it
can commence. As they weave their way through the
cartoonish landscape they will fight with their options to
either trap the Flagrant Five with their shadow guns, or
disobey their creator's orders and finally kill the Five for
good.

~**The hands of the girls were inside of each-others zip front grey boiler suits** and they sat in the blood from where Sonny's face collided with the surface. The brunette had a finger smear of it next to her mouth.

"You two sluts put each other down and go tell Moira that Sonny's done. I'm coming in, just got a little business to attend to first."

As the two started to leave the big blond grabbed the shoulder of the red head and pulled her back.

"Not you Fire-Crotch, all this fucking blood has got me going." She started to unbuckle the belt on her camouflage hot pants. "Down you go, bitch!"

~**Short stories from the Most Depraved Writer in Print.** Dark and twisted tales of exquisite violence, rough tricks, narcotics consumption, evil ghosts and drug-snuffling demons. Evil grandfathers and animal-human hybrid clones. Morbid serial killer stalking night darkened hallways of an unsuspecting hospital. Life underground following the frozen apocalypse. Tales of ancient blood-thirsty vampires and Roman decadence. Enjoy all of the hardcore, dystopic, viscerally violent stories. Not for easily offended mamby-pambies. Dark fiction at its finest.

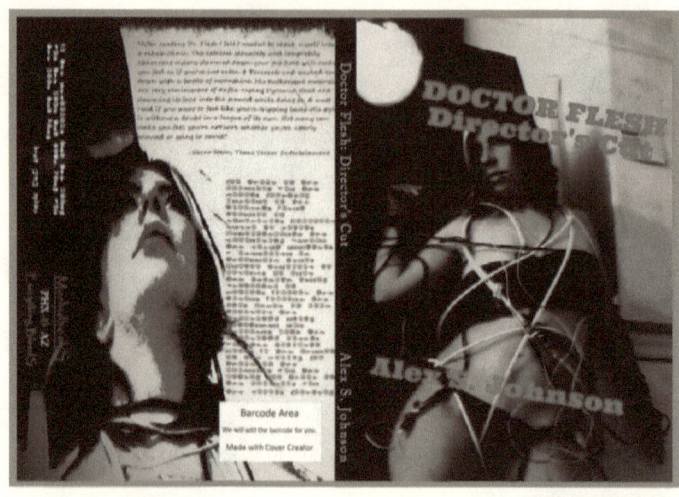

~From Alex S. Johnson, the author of Bad Sunset, Wicked Candy and The Death Jazz, comes a new vision in Bizarro horror. Imagine a TROMA film on meth and acid, one part cyberpunk, one part Franz Kafka, and three parts frankly unsuitable for a sane audience. "Will make you feel as if you've just eaten 8 Percocets and washed 'em down with a bottle of moonshine," says Necro Stein of Texas Terror Entertainment.

~When the winds blew i felt them blowing through me,
when the land shook, it was my corpus that trembled. When
the tides ebbed and flowed I became more shore and more
sea. I was day and night as the sun and moon described the
steps of their dancing within me. Just as I could see all the
world at once, I was all of these things at once, and the
motion of an entire world formed the foundation of my
stillness.

I'd travelled through the Sphere of Glammeth, descended
through the Guardian, and then through the Grey-Man,
fallen through a hole that pierced all the worlds.

~**He had to have her the moment he saw her trachea ring**. Six months later she was his lovely wife. He performed his duties as a husband and she as a wife. He tolerated a house filled with references to her late first husband and the children they had together. He put up with her prudish ways. He waited. He was patient. He planned. He was adaptable. He was rewarded over the course of a week in her basement. He turned his perverse sexual fantasies of worms and maggots and her lovely crusty trachea ring into a gruesome reality.

~A dirty shameful devil of a secret...

Something that two men share. A legacy that will shock you to your very core. One that is created not out of madness, but of the purest desire. Take a vivid journey into the mind of the killer and his biggest fan. Do you believe in evil? See the knife plunge. Lap at the wounds. Do you still? There is no rational meaning or pretty words that will hide away the darkness that the words of this found journal creates. Inside is the real truth. And it can set you free. Watch all you want. Taste what you dare not have.

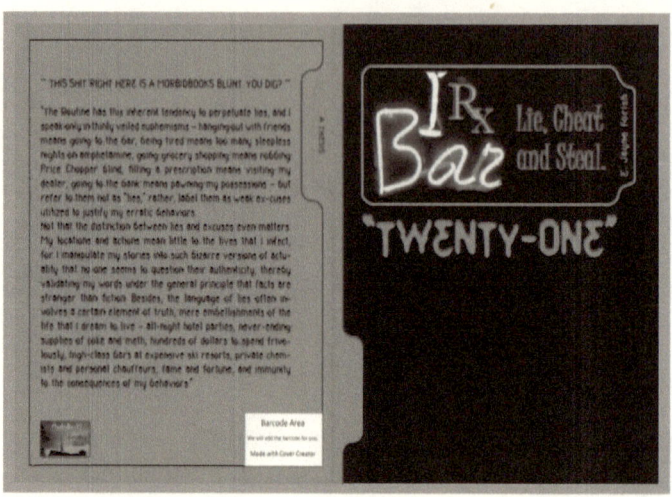

~"**The routine has this inherent tendency to perpetuate lies,** and I speak only in thinly veiled euphemisms — hanging out with friends means going to the bar; being tired means too many sleepless nights on amphetamine; going grocery shopping means robbing Price Chopper blind; filling a prescription means visiting my dealer; going to the bank means pawning my possessions — but refer to them not as "lies;" rather, label them as weak excuses utilized to justify my erratic behaviours.

~**I'm feeling down and dirty, feeling kind of mean,** so I give those fans my middle finger. Those poor bastards go nuts. My team looks at me in awe. My coach frowns and the opposing one begins to furiously scratch out new plays. I see our opponents and I almost feel sorry for the poor bastards. Their fans can't help them. Their coach can't help them. I'm going to run them off their own track in front of their own fans and there is not one thing they can do about it.

~**Humanity is the devil is a deconstructed nightmare mixing David Lynch and snuff movies.** The plot revolves around a central character, Seth, who is set about a crusade against humanity which, for him, represents pure evil. Through random killings he and his cronies try to accelerate the end of the world, in order to provoke and defeat the Demiurge, the false God that is ruling the earth. As in Burroughs, logical language is replaced here with cut-scenes – sometimes to be taken literally – that plunge the reader into an extreme experience.

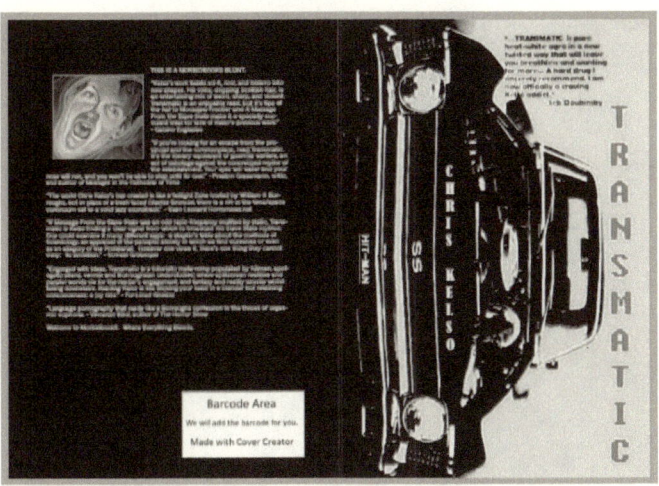

~"**As a part-time hitman/ exterminator, Ignius Ellis's dream is to buy a candy-apple red Nova Supreme.** In the process of trying to earn enough cash to make his dream come true he gets sucked into the rough world of Visitacion Valley, SF. When the tenants in his apartment complex reveal their various extracurricular activities this take an even more bizarre twist and Ellis soon becomes acquainted with the nightmarish Slave State dimension..."

~That's the last time she gets the bigger worm...

Once their flesh flakes away the angels collapse into puddles
of hissing goop and withered petals blow into them hurried
along by unseen winds. My spit looses its sweet taste to the
black flavor of ash. The glowing birds in the bright orange
sky burst into small sparkly novas. The sky itself weeps and
tears, streaking down like a ruined painting as the dismal
grey of life wheezes back before my eyes. I don't blink;
praying silently for one last desperate sensation of the high.
Lila feels it too. She writhes on the mattress next to me...

~Scary as ever.

He looked at her and grinned wickedly, the overcasting shadows of the outer corner of the stone wall, combined with the flickering light above them, created a deadly feature across the side of his face. He sees her lying helpless. He chuckled eerily, and instantly raised his hand. Her eyes widened to the sight of the gleaming sharp knife in his grasp.

He even held it up for her to see it better.

She stared up at him and then to the knife, panting in fear. Her heart pounded throughout her body as he chuckled once more saying deeply,

"Oh excellent. I've found you . . ."

~**Within these twisted and perverted pages**, Johnson manages to demolish clichés with a jaded finesse that I've personally never encountered in written form. Another apparent talent is his effortless deconstruction of pop-culture allegories and references as found in his story "Vampussy." No one is safe or spared from his dagger sharp sarcasm and wit.

While not without its flaws, my appreciation for this kind of talent and voice is what made his writing so fun to read, even if he might possibly be out of his ever-loving mind.

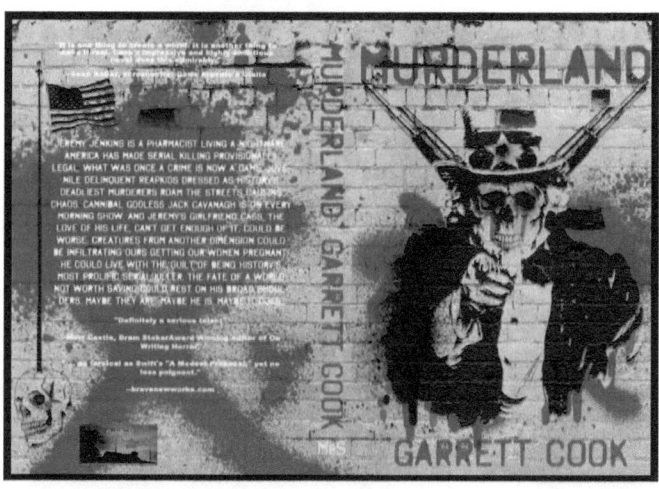

~In Garrett Cook's Murderland serial killers are idolized by society. Their deeds are followed obsessively by television pundits and the adoring public. A subculture has grown up around this phenomena, called "Reap." Laws are created to allow this activity to flourish, including designated "safe zones' where killers can practice their trade without fear of persecution. Fans of the top rated serial killers celebrate each new kill on social media and television. Programs glorify their deeds.

The culture of Murderland is violent and mirrors our own violent society and its decadent obsessions.

~Born whole from the rectum of a dying patient, Morbid silently stalks the hospital's hallways, heinously dispatching the most helpless of patients and in the most painfully repulsive of manners. In the meantime, in order to pay for his family and home that includes his ghost step-father Sammy and his pet aborted fetus Chip, Westphal has to ingest mounds of dangerous narcotics to get through his night shifts. Barely hanging on to his Care Tech gig by his fingernails, the last thing Westphal needs is to be accused of Morbid's evil deeds. You, on the other hand, simply seek some solace from all Your diseases.

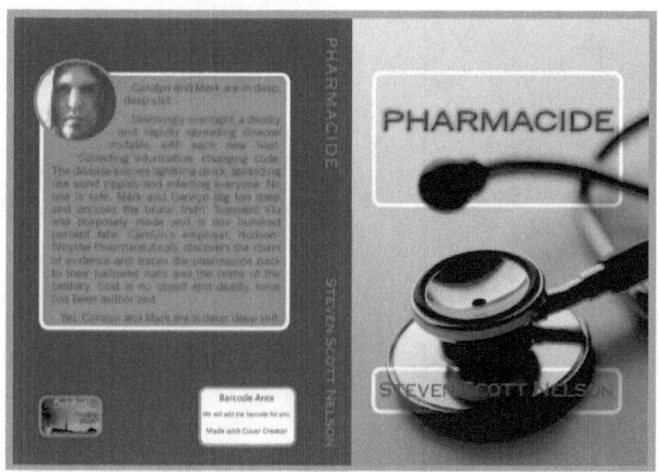

~It looks like Carolyn and Mark are in deep, deep shit...
Mark and Carolyn live in an alternate 1989 where Ronald
Reagan is on his fourth presidential term. The USA has a
rigid, long-standing caste system and abortions were never
made legal. Being homeless is a crime that is punishable by
imprisonment in Tent City. Most of Mark's ER patients are
inmates at this camp and are victims of a new disease
dubbed; Transient Flu. This deadly and rapidly spreading
disease mutates with each new host, collecting information,
changing code. The disease evolves lightning quick,
spreading like pond ripples...

~IMMANUEL THE CHRIST has some nerve. Jonah has already lost everyone he loves to Pilate the vampire and his Harbor drug violence. Jonah now trudges through his days staying as high on Plata as possible. He just wants to be left alone while he waits for his turn to die. The Christ has other plans for him. She sends Pedro, to assign Jonah to order the Herod to dismantle the Harbor's Plata trade. Jonah decides to run. But you can't run from God. As Jonah learns the hard way when the 'Edmund Fitzgerald' goes down in rough seas, with the reluctant prophet on board…

~**Five Very Wicked Shorts.** Brought to you with love and blood from The Grim Reverend Steven Rage, the 'Most Depraved Writer in Print'. ~

Through the sheer shock of his presentation, Rage forces readers to consider the alternatives, to look at the garbage in the streets, to see what is swept into the gutters at night right before all decent people awake to see another cleaned up version of the day. Depravity at its finest, but really the stories are loads of fun.

~Pontius Pilate is cursed to be a vampire. Life after life after life.~ And for the Plata dealing Pilate, his life is more like a death sentence. His only chance surviving is to keep on selling his monthly quota of Plata. This new man-made narcotic is a potent speed-ball designed to amp up the user, while also numbing the conscience into euphoric oblivion. To nullify the pain. To stifle the torture. To run and to hid from all the anguish inside. PILATE is a drug lord vampire in this re-telling of Christ's final days.

~So I, The Spun Monkey, have returned from running my errands, safe and sound. Having failed rehab once again, The Spun Monkey went ahead and procured myself an 8-ball of crispy, crunchy Columbian Bam-Bam. I chipped, chopped, lined and blasted off with two bigguns up each side. OOH OOH EEE EEE-fuckmerunning- OOH-OOH-OOH, motherfuckers! Monkey be ready... Yes, indeeeeeed.... Having had my jet fuel, I then sat my hairy asshole down at the keyboard and began flailing away. The monkey hopes you dig the fruits of my labors in 'The Spun Monkey's Digest'. And if you not ... well then ... you can go eff yourself, Capitan!

~**Following religious folklore, parables, and beliefs,** Rage presents the readers with a God who truly is the Shepherd that leaves no sheep behind. While this tale is deeply woven with the intricacies of a dark, drug-infested world ruled by evil forces, this is the story of a lost sheep. All are God's children, even the most foulest of evil creatures who by their own will have become so through their spiritual and physical copulation with the Devil, and as such, in God's mercy, still are given a chance to be saved.

~ CARGO CONTAINS:

1. *Space-wrecked on Venus* by NEIL R. JONES
2. *For All the Marbles* by REV. STEVEN RAGE
3. *Tony and the Beetles* by PHILIP K. DICK
4. *Acid Bath* by VASELEOS GARSON
5. *The Butterfly Kiss* by ARTHUR DEKKER SAVAGE
6. *The Moon Destroyers* by MONROE K. RUCH

FROM SOME OF THE GIANTS OF THE GOLDEN AGE to the darkest of dystopian noir, MorbidbookS SciFi Anthology will take you from hopeful space travel to living hand-to-mouth in the despair beneath the Earth.
Welcome to your future.

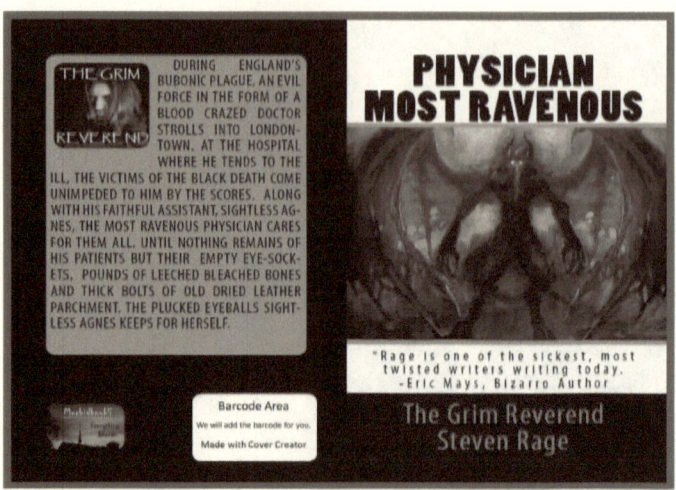

~**During the height of England's Bubonic Plague an ancient Evil Force strolls into London-Town** in the form of a would-be doctor. It could smell the blood from miles away, wanting only to help. At the hospital where he cares for the victims of this Black Death, the ill come to him unimpeded. They arrived and fell by the scores. With the help of his ever-faithful assistant, Sightless Agnes, a most ravenous cares for them all. Eating his way through an entire hospital, he treats them until there is nothing left. Nothing save their empty eye sockets, a few pounds of leeched bleached bones and some bolts of old dried-out flesh-leather parchment.

~**New from MorbidbookS; Where Everything Bleeds** is an instant collector's specimen and a certain stunner. ~ Be the first freak on your block to acquire this singular and unexpurgated exquisite culling of The Grim Reverend Steven Rage's favorite 'meds'. Enjoy this one–of–a–kind vivid look into the twisted mind of The Most Depraved Writer In Print as he captains you through the intoxicating stain of his wicked imagination. Included are numerous Photos, Paintings and Illustrations embellished with dramatic grayscale that enhance these iniquitous and magnificent Dark Fantasy fables.

~Click On Image For More MorbidbookS On Kindle~